THE MAGDALENA GAMBIT

MX Publishing

THE MAGDALENA GAMBIT

Oscar Ortiz

MX Publishing

Book #5 in the CODE NAME DELTA series

*To my son Alex Francisco,
my dear 'Big Guy'*

Must read 🏆

Praise for The Magdalena Gambit

AWARDED 4 STARS BY THE ONLINE BOOK CLUB

"The Magdalena Gambit by Oscar Ortiz is a thriller set in a political intelligence framework like the James Bond series, but with an American touch. I recommend it to lovers of spies, eliminators, and dangerous mission stories. It will also appeal to Bond enthusiasts."

A NEW KIND OF ANTI-HERO

"Ortiz's attempt to take the traditional spy thrillers' fans back to Cold War times with his new Code Name Delta series works not only because it embodies the principles of the hard-boiled detective novel, its cynicism, its veiled critique of political systems, its deep immersion in the psychological complexity of some of the characters who do not abide by the sharp dissonances between good and evil, but also because secret agent Patrick Coonan is an anti-hero who is sometimes mocked by his chief because he lacks brains and often gets by purely by chance, even though he eventually perceives the hidden plots around him. It is traits such as these that place him on a different shore of the genre. And, if the phrase fits, a fresh option to what has already been written by the big guns of this genre."

—Adriana Herrera
Literary critic of the Nuevo Herald

A SOLID CHARACTER IN AN EVER-CHANGING WORLD

"When a writer reaches the fifth novel of a character as solid and enduring as Patrick Coonan, alias Agent Delta, top

eliminator for the Quadrille, considering the coherence, erudition and narrative invested in the development of the secret agent's missions, we can affirm – without fear of being mistaken – that this author is well above good and evil. It is not necessary to have read the prior installments of the series to be able to enjoy Coonan's new adventure, although it is advisable to get a hold on them if the reader wishes to know in depth some of the characters inherited from previous episodes. At the heart of The Magdalena Gambit *lies a more melancholic treatise than expected on the survival of the tough but vulnerable man amid a changing and convulsive era."*

—*Josep Ferran Valls*
Spanish novelist and literary critic

5th BOOK IN THE CODE NAME DELTA SERIES

"Oscar Ortiz's novel, The Magdalena Gambit, *is a well-constructed example of its genre. All the key character archetypes appear, and little text is wasted on superfluous descriptions or inter-relationships. Ortiz is to the point and presents just the facts of the assignment, pertinent infodumps, and the mission's execution. Each chapter provides helpful footnotes to assist readers with foreign translations and references to the first four books. While reading the previous novels beforehand would certainly add to the richness and understanding of Coonan's world, Ortiz's straightforward storytelling and adherence to the typical spy procedural make it accessible as a standalone."*

—*Alana Maple*
Reviewer for Reedsy.com

PATRICK COONAN IN THE DOLDRUMS

"In this new Delta adventure, Oscar Ortiz takes up some of the themes already used by Ian Fleming in Thunderball, The Spy Who Loved Me, *etc... But the Berlin Wall has fallen, the Soviet empire has collapsed, thus a new world order has been established. Muslim terrorism dug its nest, the Russian Mafia and other arms dealers joined the dance, and a very somber score is composed. Now it's a question of orchestrating it without hitting the wrong notes. Patrick Coonan is once again at work in a mission where friends can quickly turn into enemies and vice versa. Ortiz describes a ruthless, morally bankrupt world where the rules of the game are quickly changing to suit the interests of the moment... More to come in the next episode!"*

—Renan Bourgeat
French reviewer for Amazon.fr

*"There are three kinds of men. The living. The dead.
And those who dwell in the sea."*

— Socrates —

TABLE OF CONTENTS

FOREWORD

(An introduction to the secret file of Patrick Coonan)

In recent times, the cinematic James Bond has been converted into a "catwalk muscleman" bearing an asphalt face and a propensity for melancholy. To escape from this new "politically correct" version of the character, incapable of being seductive and without any trace of the model developed by Ian Fleming in his novels, there still are few options available. The most obvious one is to review Fleming's books or the films starring Sean Connery and his most popular successors.

Another option is the pulp narrative alternative to 007, currently well-served by the prolific Cuban American writer Oscar Ortiz. This is the series *Code Name Delta*, starring Patrick Coonan, a U.S. Rangers' sniper transformed into a clandestine operator for the Quadrille — the sharp counterintelligence unit created by Ret. Special Forces Col. Marlon Berkowitz to safeguard America from all threats. Always with the protracted shadow of the Cold War as the background, which also served as the main setting in the first Bond book written by Fleming.

Ortiz's virtues as a novelist can be well-appreciated in all his Patrick Coonan adventures: a concise, direct prose, halfway between the noir mystery genre and the spy thriller; utmost erudition in the different topics dealt with, where one perceives a thorough work of research and the offering to the reader of varied plots that combine investigation, violent death, sexuality, and an uncomfortable background of moral sordidness.

Josep Ferran Valls
Valencia, Spain - Oct. 2022

DRAMATIS PERSONAE

ABRAMOVICH (Valentin)
Alias Heckle. Russian mercenary hired by Yuri Pavenko to protect the secret facility in Barranquilla, Colombia, where the hijacked submarine is located. He is paired with Sokolov.

AHMED (Commander)
Known only by his *nom de guerre*, Commander Ahmed is a Palestinian-born mujahideen who leads the armed wing of Islamic Sword, a group of extremist Muslims who have declared Jihad on Uncle Sam. He was posing as a double-agent for the CIA, when discovered by Pat and Jessica during Operation Scorpion Tail.

ALEDO (Margot)
Acting chief of staff for the Quadrille who also oversees CI5's Shared Archives Department. Mrs. Aledo serves as Col. Berkowitz's personal assistant in matters of administration within the CI5 headquarters.

BENSON (Bruce)
Aide-de-camp to Special Agent Samuel Norwood of the FBI's Organized Crime Division. Works as a team with Agent Greenwald.

BERKOWITZ (Marlon)
A.k.a. the Colonel. A retired U.S. Special Forces colonel, veteran of the Vietnam War and the invasion of Grenada. Founder and director of operations of the Quadrille, currently in command of CI5. Col. Berkowitz is Pat and Jessica's immediate chief.

BULL (Jackson)
Also known as Jack Bull, he is an agent of the National Reconnaissance Office, currently assigned to track down and capture black-market dealers of Weapons of Mass Destruction.

CEDEÑO (Bartolo)
General of the Colombian Army, leader of the Search Bloc (BdB). Secret ally of Colonel Berkowitz.

COCO

Barranquilla fisherman who operates on the Magdalena River. He offers, for a price, to transport Karina and Pat to the clandestine facility where the atomic sub is located.

COONAN (Patrick)

Codenamed Delta, Pat is the best eliminator under Col. Marlon Berkowitz's command: he is, also, one of Berkowitz's most loyal followers among the original Quadrille members and one the Colonel completely trusts. He is the protagonist of the series.

ELLIOT, JR. (Martin)

U.S. Navy admiral, commander of a nuclear submarine. One of the officers involved in the trafficking of Weapons of Mass Destruction.

FELDMAN (Arnold)

General Director of the Organized Crime Force (OCF). Man of intrigue and great influence in Washington political circles.

FITTS (Jessica)

Codenamed Phi. Intelligence analyst hired by the Colonel to join the new Quadrille, now operating as CI5. She is also Pat's new partner.

GREENWALD (Len)

Aide-de-camp to Special Agent Samuel Norwood of the FBI's Organized Crime Division. He teams up with Agent Benson.

JOHNSON (Bill)

Alias the Armorer. A senior member of the Quadrille now working as the official armorer for CI5. Also heads the Special Effects section of the unit.

KARMEN

Member of an elite team of contract operatives, named Triple K, the Colonel employed to support Pat and Jessica in Operation Parasol. Karina Reyes's second in command.

KODINA (Andrei)

Former chief of staff of the Atomic Fang Division of the defunct

KGB during the Soviet era and former supervisor of Yuri Pavenko when he was still a member of the KGB. Kodina is the current president of ROSONOVO-RONEXPORT, the Russian Federation's military equipment export agency under Vladimir Putin.

NORWOOD (Samuel)

A senior FBI agent currently working for the Bureau's Organized Crime Division: he specializes in the Russian Mafia. During the Cold War Norwood worked in Washington, D.C. hunting illegal spies from the former KGB. Works as a team with Greenwald and Benson.

OSTROVSKY (Oleg)

Russian mobster. Head of the feared Ostrovsky Clan, which he runs in partnership with his brother, Terek.

OSTROVSKY (Terek)

Russian mobster. Head of the feared Ostrovsky Clan, which he runs in partnership with his brother, Oleg.

PAVENKO (Yuri)

A former Soviet KGB nuclear saboteur turned into a very dangerous dealer of Weapons of Mass Destruction.

PRATT (Ernest S.)

Admiral of the U.S. Navy, commander of a nuclear submarine. One of the officers involved in the trafficking of Weapons of Mass Destruction.

REYES (Karina)

Independent operator of Mexican ancestry. Head of the Triple K Group. She is a sniper and explosives expert. Works under contract for General Cedeño and his BdB and for CI5, when she is hired by Col. Berkowitz.

SELTZER (Peter M.)

Admiral of the U.S. Navy and one of the top Joint Chiefs of the Joint Command. Friend of Col. Marlon Berkowitz and immediate superior of Admiral Fullerton.

SOKOLOV (Misha)

Alias Jeckel. Russian mercenary hired by Yuri Pavenko to protect the secret installation in Barranquilla, Colombia. Works in tandem with Abramovich.

TETRIAK (Nina)

A.k.a. Nina the Gunslinger, she is Pavenko's protégé, also his right hand in the business, his concubine and main enforcer.

TILSON (Alfred)

During the formation of the Quadrille, he was brought in by Col. Berkowitz as his second in the chain of command in the organization. He was Pat's main instructor during the selection training period.

ZAMBRANO LORA (Cesar)

Gen. Cedeño's aid-de-camp in the Colombian Search Bloc (BdB). He worked with Pat and Jessica during Operation Scorpion Tail, in Cali.

*P*rologue

In 1997, agents from the Federal Bureau of Investigation (FBI), working in tandem with the Drug Enforcement Administration (DEA), discovered — and prevented — the sale of a Russian nuclear sub destined to be used as an underwater mule by the Cali Cartel. The transaction was valued at thirty-five million dollars and the Feds charged Ludwig Fainberg of Brighton Beach, N.Y. (a Russian mobster nicknamed "Tarzan") who ended up relocated to Miami, as the promoter of the deal. "Tarzan," who in addition to being a businessman and a gangster was quite an affable guy, candidly confessed that all he had to do to make the purchase was dial the number of his contact in St. Petersburg and ask him if there was a possibility of acquiring a military submarine. His contact responded with another question: *"How do you want it, with or without the missiles?"* When the news spread like wildfire throughout the globe, it made many of us aware of the existing corruption and laxity in the Russian arsenals, inherited from the Soviet Union.

A few years after, in September of 2000, Mr. Leo Arreguin (the DEA director in Colombia) attested to another sub that had been discovered half-built, and confiscated by the Colombian authorities in Facatativa, a municipality in the Department of Cundinamarca that lies only thirty-one kilometers from the Colombian Capital of Bogota. This submarine measured thirty-six meters in length by four meters in draft and was ready to be moved by land in three caps to the Pacific. Right after this shocking discovery, another one was made: a submarine factory established in a warehouse located at Kilometer 30, on the road that leads from Bogota to Facatativa; it is deduced that the racket was set up especially to supply organized crime outfits. According to the preliminary investigations, the potential buyers of these custom-made subs would be the major drug cartels, in their struggle to move large shipments between one hundred and fifty to two hundred tons of cocaine. But the agents who participated in the operation found documents in Cyrillic and construction manuals in Russian. If at any time there was hesitation about the involvement of the Russian Mob — which I doubt, of course — the police attaché of the new Russian Federation in Colombia, who openly confessed that at first he believed that they were pulling his leg, declared before the press: *"This technology comes from my country,"* when it became known that, in addition to the technical manuals, there were Russian tools that bore the emblem of the hammer and sickle, an unmistakable symbol of the Soviet regime.

However you look at it, the birth of a black-market industry to produce custom-built subs upon demand from any bidder with enough dough to pay for them is a direct threat to global security ... and raises a disturbing query: *What will happen when Colombia's guerrilla groups, or any other extremists from around the world acquire attack subs?*

The discovery of Facatativa not only worried officials in the high echelons of the Colombian government, but also in ours as well, and many other Western powers, prompting us all to take swift and drastic measures. But the news also generated sinister ideas in the minds of third parties, unscrupulous people regardless of their nationality or side, with enough resources and the appropriate connections to continue taking advantage of the lack of control that this New World Order seems to have brought upon us. One of them, naturally, was Yuri Pavenko: dealer extraordinaire of those weapons known today by the acronym WMD.

The Weapons of Mass Destruction.

But as it turned out, Yuri Pavenko was not the only one....

ENIGMA 3

Part One

THE MISSING SUBS

I said, "With all due respect, sir, it's bullshit," and I said this in harsh conviction. "I've never believed that theory, not even during my youth, when the topic was in vogue during the 1970s."

My disdainful comment won me a sour grin. Marlon Berkowitz was not a man given to tolerate vulgarity among his minions, but in this circumstance, he had no choice but to put up with what some at headquarters call an "irritating personality" — mine, that is. Col. Marlon Berkowitz, still supreme commander and Chief Director of Operations at CI5 (that's Counterintelligence No. 5, to you) had sent for me to ask a favor.

"So, you don't believe in the myth of the Bermuda Triangle?"

"Absolutely not, sir. It was proven to be just that, a myth. The disappearances of all the crafts involved, both aerial and maritime, were more the product of modern pirates, drug traffickers and kidnappers than of imaginary extraterrestrial beings and mysterious magnetic fields..."

"Well, that's the idea, isn't it?" He pointed out, without letting me carry the sentence to completion. "That's the angle I wish to explore."

"The angle you wish to explore... I see." I repeated

after him before taking a long breath and shrugging my shoulders. "Very good, sir. I'm all ears."

That was when he started the briefing. In recent months, the U.S. Navy had lost three nuclear submarines with more than enough power on board to devastate the world, not once, but ten times over. A *very* serious matter, I must add. We had become the laughingstock of the planet, having spent years criticizing the Russians for being so "careless and irresponsible" with their nuclear arsenal... And now it seemed *we* were the ones endangering all of humanity if one of these formidable weapons created and manufactured by us fell into the wrong hands. Fortunately, two of the three missing subs had already been located by Naval Intelligence, but the third — the largest and most dangerous of the trio — had not yet been placed in safekeeping. Let us take into consideration that, at the time all this went down, we were entering the third millennium, with a New World Order where (unfortunately) terrorists ruled the roost... Therefore, I wondered, what angle was Col. Berkowitz referring to.

"I'm sorry, Pat," my chief said, "I have no right to drag you into this mess, but it fell right into my lap for being in the wrong place at the wrong time."

"That's usually the way shit happens, sir," I mumbled, and he heard me. He just pretended he hadn't.

The fact that he'd called me by my first name, while we were both sitting in his office at CI5 headquarters in Midtown Miami, could not be overlooked; it was *significant*. Both in that office, and in all the others he'd had in different places throughout our work association, I'd always been Delta to him, a code name he himself had assigned to me for almost two decades now.

"Perhaps if you would deign to tell me everything there is about the matter, just for once in your life," I dropped with a hint of sarcasm, "it would be easier for me to accept what you're asking of me... How the hell did you let yourself get mixed up in this, sir? As far as I know, CI5 is not a spook shop, quite the opposite, and the Navy has a vast Intelligence Department; a *very* competent one, I should add. You even mentioned that they have already located two..."

"I know, I know," he admitted sternly. "Anyway, here goes the story. The week I spent in Washington, I was invited to a dinner at the Pentagon, given in honor of one of the Joint Chiefs."

"Wow... Let me guess, sir: the Chief of Naval Operations," I ventured.

He grinned sourly at my voluntary observation, as if to say "obviously" and then he continued with his story.

"Admiral Peter M. Seltzer and I served together in the Navy SEALs during the Vietnam War, when I was a captain in the U.S. Special Forces, and we are good friends of long standing. After the ceremony, he invited me over for a couple of drinks at his house in a quiet Maryland suburb, and he told me a story as fascinating as it is incredible... Have you heard of the *Akula*?"

"Yes, I have. A Russian attack submarine," I hastened to answer his question. "That's all I know, sir."

"Very well. The *Akula* class was built in the 1980s with a single purpose: to hunt down American nuclear subs. I understand that it is a technological marvel, with a navigation system that is undetectable under the sea. 'Undetectable' is the key word in this story."

"I'm not impressed by Soviet technology, sir. They were masters at mass production of scrap metal when they were a world superpower, but now..."

"They have improved *significantly*," he said. "We're facing the proof of that today, three American submarines missing without a chance to fight back."

"And the Joint Chiefs think that an *Akula* is responsible, isn't that it?

"Or more than one; the Russian Navy has almost twenty of the darned things operating in international waters."

"I refuse to believe it, Colonel," I said, emphatically shaking my head. "We were always the king of the oceans, for many years our fleet of *Polaris* was the detente that prevented Soviet Russia from attacking us.

"Certainly, this is where Vladimir Putin's obsession with surpassing us comes from. You know that, aside from being Prime Minister of Russia since '99, the man is a former KGB operative."

"A minor one, I'm told." I spoke.

"Don't underestimate him, Delta. He didn't have the chance back then to work his way up to threat-to-the-West level, but that's because the Empire collapsed on him. Putin is a man to watch out for, trust me."

"Even *after* the fall of the Soviet regime and the end of the Cold War? Mm... Come on, Colonel!"

He didn't respond to my disdainful skepticism, he just nodded his head, as if approving, and remained silent for a few more seconds. But I, somewhat uncomfortable with his silence, urged him to continue with his story.

"I'm not ruling out the possibility that the Russians have returned to their old evil ways," he said, "but I don't share the idea that they have achieved technological supremacy on the seas, yet. I think that *someone*, somewhere, is being very clever and tricky. That's what I told Admiral Seltzer."

"Ah!" I exclaimed in mild reproach. "That's what one gets for handing out opinions...."

"Yes, I know, that was my mistake. The Admiral was impressed with my theory, and, given the desperation and embarrassment caused by the loss of his nuclear subs, he asked me to explore that angle."

"Which one?" I asked to prod him, "The one about magnetic fields?"

"I never said that, Pat; I am inclined towards the theory that they want to convince us of their invincibility to put fear in our souls and force us to waste resources on unbridled defensive measures."

"Like old Reagan did with the Soviets when he threatened them with the Star Wars project, isn't it?

"You mean the Space Defense Initiative, but yes, that's it. More or less."

"Then you think it's a farce."

"Negative, the threat is tangible, but I do not think it is conceived as the Joint Chiefs imagine it."

"Let's see, sir, why don't you explain it to me?"

In response, he pushed the talk-button on the Intercom and ordered: "Mrs. Aledo, is Agent Phi in the building?"

"Yes, sir, she is in her office," was the rigid response from his chief of staff.

"Send her right up, will you? Immediately. We are waiting for her."

"Right away, sir."

"Thank you."

Naturally, things started to get complicated after my partner Jessica arrived very willing to lecture us on the subject. In the beginning of her Excel presentation, I could hardly focus on what she had to say, it was all naval gibberish that I don't understand, and all I did was stare at her with the repressed desire of the many weeks we had been apart; *months* without even sharing a mission with her. After Operation Parasol, the Colonel had put up a wall between us; but Phi wasn't showing any signs of having missed my company, so, if she were feeling the same as me, she hid it very well. In fact, she looked relaxed, professional, and excited about this new project. So, I thought *fuck it* and did my best to focus on the matter at hand.

As expected, being the team's analyst and all, she came well-prepared to give one of her detailed lectures on the latest naval maneuvers of the Russians and Chinese in waters near the American continent. She spoke in depth about the various types of submarines that the Russian Federation has, and the progress made by their scientists in silencing their ships for underwater warfare. I thought about everything she said, you know... Firstly, because I don't understand a damn thing about those topics and, secondly, because I never swallowed the pill that the former Soviets have gotten so far ahead of us. I'm not as dumb as some at headquarters think, I read the Department of Defense statistics from time to time and the last time I did (just two or three months ago) the United States of America was still ahead in the defense spending budget. We invested a lot more on war toys and tech gadgets than the Chinese and the Russians did.

It is quite true that in the 1970s they came up with a very dangerous missile, a submarine-killer rocket christened *Sea Serpent*, which, in fact, kept the Pentagon hawks in check, overwhelmed as they were by so many cuts in the national defense budget imposed by the administration of former President Jimmy Carter. But with the coming to power of the old Reagan the tables were turned and very soon their *Sea Serpent* became obsolete when the U.S. Navy put into production an anti-rocket missile baptized with the no less suggestive name of *Mongoose*. And that was it; our *Mongoose* ate up the Russian *Sea Serpent* and the United States regained its status as 'king of the deeps' in underwater warfare.

Jessica emphasized the mysterious appearances of a Russian vessel in the waters of the Gulf of Mexico whose discovery had caused the head of the Southern Command, relocated to Key West after the Panama Canal ceased to be a possession of ours, to react, prompting a maneuver in which our three missing subs had participated.

So, when the Colonel brought the case to me, there was already a definite pattern, the submarines disappeared in sets of three. One vanished in the Pacific; one in the North Atlantic; one in the Caribbean... But there were other relevant details that were not brought to the table by Jessica, but by my boss.

"I have pondered the matter, and I am almost convinced that there is a catch here. I insist that someone is trying hard to make us believe that the *Akulas* are invincible."

I said nothing so as not to spoil his party, but his observation was more than obvious to me.

"There are more common denominators in all the disappearances," interjected Jessica.

"Let me guess," I said, unable to hold back this time, "the link lies with the ships' commanders."

The Colonel looked me in the eye, and I thought I noticed the outcropping of a fleeting mischievous smile on those thin, cruel-looking lips.

Jessica was shocked to realize that I had just batted the ball out of the field.

"What did you say?!"

"If they weren't bought," I continued undaunted, "they have been extorting them in some way to have their ships wrecked or delivered to God knows what remote wastelands of the globe to be dismantled and thus disappear."

"Are you aware of what you are implying, Delta?" sparked Jessica. "Traitorous admirals in the U.S. Navy?"

"For Christ's sake, why not, Phi? Didn't the Rosenbergs sell the secret of the atomic bomb to the Reds? And that son-of-a-bitch Aldrich Ames our most precious secrets to the Russians? Traitors have always existed everywhere! In our capitalist society the main motivation has always been profit."

"But not the only one," pointed out the Colonel taking up the lead. "There is another powerful motive, and you know it as well as I do because it has touched us closely. Resentment."

He was now making a direct allusion to Alfred Tilson's case. The man who'd been his second in command in the Quadrille during the Cold War and all the years after being disbanded in 1992. Old Al had been our Master instructor, and one of the finest government assassins I ever met, but he had tired of being Marlon Berkowitz's right-hand man in the organization....

I could not help but experience a painful flashback, suddenly triggered by the Colonel's allusion to that sad incident, back in Aruba during Operation Parasol, in which Tilson's treachery forced me to prepare the conditions for his execution. Normally, when I'm ordered to eliminate someone, I do it without remorse. It's my job, I'm a trained eliminator and I'm good at it. But Tilson and I had been close — well, as close as one can get in this racket of ours. He'd been my initial trainer and also my executive director in the field in one of the most dangerous missions I undertook with the Quadrille, the first time I was ordered by the Colonel to remove someone outside the country, behind the Iron Curtain.

The memories were very vivid and coming in now, my mind flying back to Aruba. Tilson and I facing each other in the office he was using as a front in Oranjestad, the place from where he managed a team of twelve OCF operatives under his command, now that he was no longer working directly with us but had become a liaison officer between our CI5 subsection and the general director of the OCF, Mr. Arnold fuckin' Feldman. I remember him leaving the chair behind his desk growling through clenched teeth while taking steps in the direction of the wooden cabinet, where he kept his liquor. At no time did he turn his back on me, not even once, as he reached for another bottle of whiskey. The semi-auto SW22 pistol firmly clutched in his right hand.

"Where the hell are Karina and her crew?"

I remember thinking that frightening moment when my life depended on the efficiency and punctuality of the Triple K operatives my boss had hired to carry out the hit. He suspected that, regardless of my acceptable track record and long experience, I would not be the best suited for this job and, of course, he was right. He always was. But Tilson had taken the lead and had come for me when I least expected it and now, I was helpless, and in no position to counterattack. It seemed as if I was entirely dependent on the accuracy of whoever was out there with a powerful long-range rifle.

Well, it was becoming obvious that I'd better come up with other plans rather than waiting for my "saving angels" to shoot the target. Instinct forced me to jump on the desk and try to seize the Ruger he'd taken away from me, or reach out for the pocketknife, which now rested on his desk surface. But an inner voice warned me that I would never make it, not with Tilson as an adversary, who was a true master in the killing arts. The shotgun was out of my reach, that much I knew, he'd left it leaning against the far wall.

Then I'd seen the beam coming out of nowhere like an

unexpected miracle. A thin dot of red light landed like a silent wasp on old Al's back, sliding down it until it stopped right between his shoulder blades.

"What you've told to me," I said to keep him distracted, "is quite shocking. Peculiar, isn't it?

"Did you say *peculiar*, lad?" He snapped. *What* is peculiar?"

"The message you just passed on to me: *That* is peculiar. The reason I find this odd is because someone else also gave me a message for you."

This made him pause in his hunt for alcohol and tune up his ears. I prayed to God that he would not turn to face the window now. So, I struggled to keep all his attention focused on me.

"You are a funny guy, you know?" he said with a twisted grin. "What message are you talking about, Patrick?"

"The one sent to you by a gentleman named... Well, let's just call him Mr. B."

"Mr. B? Oh, I get it, you mean your boss, the Colonel?" He said and the grin evolved into a grimace. "Well, he can go rot in hell!"

"Do you want to hear what he has to say, or not?" I persisted in keeping him busy.

"Sure, why not, spit it out... Now, where the *fuck* is that bottle, dammit!"

The red dot oscillated slightly, and I realized I'd better hurry, or soon he wouldn't be in condition to hear me out. Whoever was behind the scope out there was calculating the distance of the shot against the wind speed, the angle of the gun's position and the force of the rifle's recoil. I had no idea what gun they were using, and I really didn't care if they could hit the mark.

"Come on, sport, spit out your little message. What did the old fox order you to tell me, huh?"

"Here you go, *buddy*," I said, mimicking his odious New England accent to perfection, "you must learn not to monkey with the axe..."

My timing was perfect. The window cracked at first but then it exploded into a myriad shard. Next came the noise of the glass shattering, making me jump.

One shot was all it took, just one. It really was a spectacular performance. One moment Tilson was standing in front of the cabinet, and the next instant he was lying sprawled on the floor. I'm sure the man never knew what hit him. The sniper's bullet pierced his spine, ripping his soul away from his body in a flash.

For a few moments I felt sorry for the man who, although he'd become a traitor, was one of the most solid pillars on which my formation in the Quadrille was based. I recalled him standing tall, his back erect and a self-assured grin brightening his features next to Col. Berkowitz in front of the entire class, that night when he addressed all recruits for the first time to tell us about his unconventional specialty.

"Delta, are you listening?" The Colonel's dry voice cracked like whiplash.

I shook my head and said: "Sorry, sir. Of course I'm listening. I was just turning something in my head. You were saying?"

"Maybe you haven't noticed it, but the life of a sub commander is no life... If they are married, they lose the marriage sooner or later. Their children grow up away from their father. They miss all, or almost all, the important events in the family calendar. They are condemned to live a parsimonious, lonely and harsh existence; always waiting for the order to destroy the world at any moment. I started investigating in that vein and I've managed to gather some details that strengthen my hypothesis of foul play in the disappearances."

"Don't tell me, sir, there is a conspiracy of resentful officers within the Navy!"

More than a statement, it was a shot in the dark, on my part; deep down I never intended my saying seriously, for one thing is an isolated traitor in any of the three branches of our armed forces and another, very different, by the way, is a plot. That only happens in Third World countries and some of the former Soviet republics. To even suggest it could also happen in America was pure nonsense and it came as a great surprise to me that my attempt to lighten up the meeting with a tasteless joke wrung a blunt affirmation out of him.

"You hit the nail right on the head," he laughed. "The three admirals are plotting."

Chapter 2

THE THEATRE OF OPERATIONS

Jessica's computer expertise was a categorical factor in planning the operation; it was she and my boss who put together the scheme for that project of his. It would be the first time, throughout all the missions in which I was involved with CI5, that I began to notice the undergoing change in this new version of our old Quadrille, in which the Colonel had always been the only head and all the rest of us — and by *us* I mean all his eliminators — limited ourselves to comply with the old man's orders, without questioning them or taking part in the analyzation process on which he based his strategy for each case. But that was precisely why he'd brought Jessica on board, wasn't it? To reform his new Quadrille for the XXI Century. He'd explained his reasons to me that moment of past glory, a few years back, when he'd been told by Attorney General Jo Ann Woods-Renault and some members of the Senate, that the Quadrille was back in the game, although now under the Department of Justice to fight the Russian Mafia — not part of the Department of Defense like in the old days of the Cold War — and under close supervision of Mr. Arnold Feldman from the OCF. My chief had not liked this, and neither had I, but it was a start of sorts, and "something" is better than "nothing". Right?

"I've been lucky, Delta," he'd said, "there's this young lady named Jessica Fitts who happens to be an MIT graduate. She filled out an application for employment first with the FBI and then with the OCF last month but was flatly rejected by both agencies."

At that moment I'd failed to see the motive for the good fortune he was claiming to have, but I refrained from voicing it because the note of enthusiasm in his voice was obvious, and I did not think it was wise to spoil the fun for him. This show of emotions was strange in a man not at all comfortable with baring his feelings in front of underlings. But this time, his optimism was showing, oh, yes, although I couldn't see why.

"MIT, sir? What the hell is that?"

He sighed at my blatant demonstration of the highest ignorance, but was very careful not to hurt my feelings by pointing it out, at least not that time, because our association was not yet official and much of the burden of the struggle to return to being the Quadrille now rested upon my shoulders... What can I say, even idiots have been known to be indispensable at some critical point.

"I'm referring to the Massachusetts Institute of Technology, Delta, MIT for short," he explained, "it's a private university in Cambridge with a great national reputation."

"I see, something like Harvard."

"More or less, but with some variations. The IQ required, no longer to graduate from MIT, but to be admitted as a student, is extremely high..."

"So, this young lady you mentioned must be a brain," I interrupted him, "and yet you say she's been rejected by both the FBI and the OCF. Why?"

He didn't answer that, of course.

"Someone brought her to my attention, and I took the risk of reaching out to her — I don't even know why I did it, I've never had analytical minds among the troops because it is counterproductive in this kind of operation. When I give an order, I don't need anyone to analyze it, do you understand? I just need an agent to carry it out. I take care of the analysis."

"Maybe that's why she got rejected on both counts," I reflected, thinking how different the Quadrille's recruitment rules were from those of the FBI and the CIA, which, in the case of the Bureau, only hired law students and, in the case of the Company, just recruited the know-it-alls from the most prestigious universities around the country. I thought that Miss Fitts — being so analytical, as my boss assured me — would be better off hooking up with Langley, our unit was a sordid swamp, not a sophisticate enough environment for the privileged minds of the nation. The Quadrille was formed by agents of brawn and quick wits — not to mention unscrupulous entities. But I refrained from making any scathing comments that I might regret. Something in the tone of his voice said he was determined to recruit this young lady.

Presently, the Colonel drew a long breath and said: "Times are changing, Delta, and whoever is not proficient with computers in today's world is at a disadvantage."

"I don't know shit about computers and I'm not doing so bad myself, sir," I said with the intention of stinging him a bit. "In fact, neither do you."

"True, but for a field agent to be successful in today's theater of operations, it requires analysts who can find and interpret the data used by the director of operations to organize the missions."

"Touché," I admitted and dropped the subject.

Only that, as was always his habit, he took advantage of the inclination shown by his new blonde Wonder Woman — she'd been a redhead before, if you must know — to meddle in field work as well. Nothing like gaining experience in the theater of operations to apply it to planning. Understanding all that began to take over my brain in slow but persistent waves. Somehow, intuitively and viscerally, my mind began to tie up the loose ends that eventually led me to see clearly what was unfolding before my eyes and that only the Colonel was planning. I don't think Jessica had a clue of what was going on until the time of old Marlon Berkowitz's death.

The longer you survive in my world, the more susceptible and suspicious you become of those around you, and you begin to think that the masters you've served for so long don't really value you as much as they should, your character grows sour and it becomes more and more difficult to obey the bloody orders that come from "the top" and that make no freakin' sense to the simple-minded soldier who is assigned to carry them out... Well, it's only logical that they don't, of course, because they never give you all the details, so you don't fully understand what the mission overview is, they purposely exclude you because they must stick to their bloody rules. One in particular, the need to know. The thing is, I too, although I struggled to control myself, began to experience certain symptoms of rebellion against that tenet... Let's call it the "Tilson Syndrome," to say the least, which seemed to be the very same bug that had bitten Admiral Fullerton and his confreres. Except for those who betrayed us purely and simply for the sake of profit, of course. The problem with that is that the price you pay for rebellion, if caught red-handed, is your life.

In any case, this task that the Colonel dropped on me like a hot potato on my lap, was entered into CI5's Archives by Mrs. Aledo as *Project: Enigma 3.* Mind you I call it a "project," and not "operation." My boss's personal projects, I should clarify, are direct actions not officially sanctioned by our government employer, the DOD. They were usually exchanged favors or courtesy gestures extended to other sister agencies in the vast universe of the American clandestine ops. Therefore, the illustrious names of these treacherous gents were all electronically sent to my tablet as an active file under Priority Code One. Martin Elliott, Jr., Ernest S. Pratt and Oscar Fullerton. All three U.S. Navy admirals and each in charge of a nuclear-powered attack sub. As I read their names silently and considered the top rank these men held within the Navy, I couldn't help but ponder that if our British cousins ever learned of this, they would end up dispensing us the same spiteful disdain that we had heaped on them when the former KGB snuck into their own Secret Intelligence Service, MI6 for short, during "The Cambridge Five" affair.

But, hey, nobody is perfect.

The first two of the trio I was able to discreetly eliminate before they could fully carry out the schemes they'd orchestrated, and their respective ships were recovered by two Navy SEAL teams before they ended on the black market. But Oscar Fullerton managed to escape me, and, because of him, I found myself entangled in a far-fetched race against the clock that once again would take me to the outskirts of Hell and to cross swords with the most dangerous weapons dealer who ever closed ranks with the Russian Mafia.

I bet you can probably guess who that was....

Days later, I arrived in Santiago de Cali like a crocodile arriving at a baseball game; completely disoriented. I did not even know for sure the reason for my new journey to Colombia, although it was to be expected that it was linked to the Colonel's little project in which he had emmeshed us all.

Walking out of the customs building, I took the satellite phone Bill Johnson had given me in Miami and used it to report my arrival to the CI5 Regional Control Officer in the Cauca Valley — if we had one preparing the conditions for my arrival, that is — as had been the case in the previous operation on the island of Aruba. But then I wondered who this new man would be, now that Tilson was no longer with us to exercise the same convenient functions of that time.

"This is Delta," I identified myself over the phone when I heard someone take the call, "my flight just landed. I'm at Palmaseca's waiting for instructions.

On the other end of the line, a familiar voice said: "If you look around, you will be able to locate a cab that is waiting for you. The driver should be holding up a sign with the word TRANS printed on it. Can you spot it?"

"Got it." I answered, shocked by the fact that being CI5's head of operations my boss had deigned to fly all the way down to Colombia to be my executive director in the field. Let me clarify that this was not the first time he had done so; we'd both been together in the so-called Land of the Flowers not too long ago, during Operation Scorpion Tail*, following orders from our General Director, Mr. Feldman. But I've already said that this was Col. Marlon Berkowitz's project, not an assignment ordered by the head of the Organized Crime Force, or the hawks of the Department of Defense, so his presence should not have taken me by surprise. Nonetheless, it did, and for a moment I was speechless.

The second shock I got that night, an even more stunning one, was to recognize him as the TRANS cab driver. I almost laughed in his face when I saw him in costume; I was not used to seeing him in the field. All my interactions with the Colonel in all my years with the Quadrille were transacted with both of us sitting across from each other at opposite ends of a conference table, or a desk; usually his.

A short time later we found ourselves in the room of a hotel called Las Mercedes, which seemed curiously familiar to me, considering that I had only been to Cali once before this occasion. But I immediately remembered that it had been at Las Mercedes where Jessica, the Colonel and I had held a planning session to lower the boom on old Yuri Pavenko, for misbehaving in the land of sugar cane and flowers, rum and salsa. That all turned out to be a big sham, of course, but I didn't know it then.

The Colonel stripped off the beret he wore to cover his round bald head and casually welcomed me; on his shaven scalp reflected the endemic amber light that set the room, and I noticed that his inseparable briarwood pipe hung from one end of his mouth, still unlit.

"Sit down, Delta," he seemed to invite, but it was an order, "make yourself comfortable."

"Thank you, sir. How are things going?" I asked, plopping down into a chair. "I was already wondering who would meet me in Colombia, truth is I never expected to find you here."

He grinned, and I noticed that he resembled an alien with that shaved skull of his, while his face with round glasses and thin metal frames remained submerged in the semi-darkness of the room. The dim lighting that engulfed the chamber added a ghostly touch that gave him the looks of a sleepy old dragon resting in his den, but he was not dozy, mind you, quite the contrary. He was more alive and aware than ever, because we were about to embark on one of his complicated intricacies — I realized this when I noticed the way his blue, glaucous eyes sparkled in the shadows, like those of an Eskimo dog — and we could both feel the same tingling in the pit of our stomachs that announces the beginning of a new operation. Or, in this case, of a new project.

"Fate brings us back to Colombia, eh" he said.

"So it seems, Colonel... May I smoke?" I asked.

"You may," he nodded, "we all must die of something, won't we?

I made a thank-you gesture and lit a cigarette.

"A drink?" he inquired, and I began to like his project because he treated me much better in situations like this one than when I was handling a regular assignment.

"Yes, thank you. Double Scotch on the rocks, sir."

"On its way," he replied and poured it for me with feigned kindness, of course, because he was already starting to get impatient, and I could sense that the role of the accommodating host was growing small on him. But a bitter spoonful, when handed out to someone who did not ask for it, must be sweetened up with honey, right? So, he poured me the drink just as I asked.

"We, uh..." he began speaking slowly, "we have located the missing submarine in Barranquilla, Pat."

"Admiral Fullerton's, right?" I spoke.

"Correct. As you know, the previous one we recovered belongs to the Los Angeles Class and is one hundred meters long by ten meters wide. But this one is much bigger, Pat, and an NRO satellite has detected the shipyard where it's located; it lies on the Atlantic coast of the country, in a deep grotto at the bottom of the Magdalena River. It is a gigantic ship."

"I know, an Ohio-class sub, I believe Jessica said."

"That's right. The Ohio-class is the largest in size among all the various types we have in our arsenal."

"I recall the schematics, sir," I said to poke him a little, and establish that Jessica, Agent Phi, wasn't the only one aware of the mission details, "one hundred and seventy meters long by thirteen meters wide, surface displacement: sixteen thousand tons; submerged displacement: eighteen thousand tons. Speed: twelve knots on the surface and twenty knots in submerged state. Conventional armament: one hundred and fifty-four *Tomahawk* cruise missiles and a variable quantity of regular torpedoes..."

"Enough of that," he interrupted me by raising a hand, a gesture that made me grin. "You're going to take care of neutralizing the threat, Pat. You're also going to take out the Russian mercenaries who oversee security at the shipyard where Fullerton's sub is lodged; there may be another group involved, I don't know for sure. But the mercenaries work for Yuri Pavenko, remember him?"

The question came loaded with that sly sarcasm that was usual in him, because he knew very well that I did remember; how could I forget, the old bastard had been forcing me to protect Yuri P. against all odds since the bloody Russian reappeared in Colombia as a black market dealer of Weapons of Mass Destruction, after we all thought him dead for so many years. The truth is that Pavenko was like a closet monster that haunts kids at bedtime. The monster in the Black Lagoon. His grandfather had been a career military man, an honors graduate of the Frunze Academy and a decorated hero of World War II. His father had not followed in his old man's footsteps because he'd had a bohemian and liberal spirit, but little Yuri had inherited the WWII veteran's bellicosity, although unlike his grandpa he chose not to pursue a career in the army.

After completing the mandatory period of military service, Pavenko left the ranks of the Red Army to join the infamous KGB. When Prime Minister Andropov gave the order to neutralize the threat posed to Moscow by Ronald Reagan's *Pershing II* missiles, the Soviet Intelligence capos approved the activation of the Atomic Fang, a division of nuclear sabotage specialists that infiltrated every major American coastal city for the purpose of smuggling, arming, and detonating portable nuclear bombs within our country. Yuri Pavenko was one of them.

"Perhaps you don't know it," my boss went on, "because you haven't had a chance to review the final report on the Caribbean operation that Jessica uploaded in our archives; you never read them anyway unless you're ordered to, and I doubt very much that the way things went south at Eagle Beach she had time to share this information with you. But Yuri Pavenko showed up in Aruba the same night everything went off the rails."

"What?!" I cried out, unable to hide my surprise.

"You heard me. He showed up with Nina as escort and two new gunmen working for him. There are rumors that they are Russian mercenaries who belong to the Wagner Group — or *Grupa Vagnera*, as the Russians call it."

"Really? And what was that son of a bitch doing down there?"

"What they all do, Pat, launder their dirty money. He was probably making the arrangements to transfer his proceeds from the sale of the submarine we're going to destroy. We're talking close to five million dollars here. Jessica ran into Nina on her way out of the Casino, but since she was being chased by some very nasty *boyeviks* — Russian slang to define an enforcer in the Russian

Mafiya — in charge of security down there, she was unable to find out more. Seeing the commotion that ensued, Pavenko panicked and opted to make himself vanish. That's what he normally does when the going gets rough; we both know how elusive the fat bastard is." He grinned, looking me in the eye.

"Oh, yeah," I mumbled, "we do... But wait a minute, Colonel, did I just hear you say we're going to destroy Fullerton's sub? Why not retrieve it and return the darned thing to its rightful owner: the U.S. Navy?"

"Because the DOD thinks it's time to give a good rebuke to all those who're tempted to trade in armaments of this magnitude. We want them to realize how far we're willing to go to stop this bloody WMD trafficking, Pat, we will *not* tolerate that they make a profit at the expense of putting the rest of the world at risk!"

I stared at him for a couple of seconds before raising an eyebrow, he was growing a bit cantankerous in his old age. Shoveling an ice cube into my mouth with calculated temperance, I stated, "Somehow, I find that hard to believe."

"Why? A harsh example must be set. Don't you think?"

"Forget it, sir, I'm not paid to think; my duty is to carry out your orders. Now, getting back to Yuri, I also find it hard to believe he showed up in Aruba."

"Why?"

"Because Goriainov spoke to me before I took him down, Colonel, he even hinted that old Yuri P. had died at my hands in Colombia.

"I see. Well, you know how false rumors spread in this twist of ours, and I'm sure Pavenko himself fed them so the Ostrovskys would leave him alone. The Russians never underestimated the power of disinformation...."

"True. But even so, Colonel, I don't see the logic of it. Why bother setting up the charade, only to show up there in person?"

"There's a catch. Jessica believes it's another one of his wily ruses."

"Jessica thinks that because she doesn't know *you* as well as I do..." I hissed. Those rumors had probably been spread by my boss himself to buy time and space to maneuver for his new informant.

"If you allow it, of course, I'll gladly put him down this time, he's long overdue, sir," I said, knowing that my chief wouldn't approve, "I'll get them both, Pavenko and Nina. That she-devil almost killed me in Juanchito, and she gave Jessica a good beating. If they show up at the well where that Ohio Class submarine is being held hostage, I'll take them out, Colonel... By God, I will!"

Who is being cantankerous now? I thought and held back a smile.

"You will do *nothing*, Delta." He hissed rather stiffly, and I didn't overlook how the "Pat" from only seconds before morphed into my old Quadrille code name, which again placed the authority on his side; he was giving me a direct order now. "I'll be the first to give you the go-ahead when the time comes, believe me. But I still need that pair alive. Your priorities in this case are Fullerton and his men, if they are all there, the submarine and the Russian mercenaries..."

"Is that all, sir?" I interjected sarcastically and lit another cigarette; of course, I immediately regretted opening a window for him to add more targets to the list.

"Repeat: Forget about Nina and Yuri for the time being; what interests me most is to find Admiral Fullerton, deal with him, and sabotage the submarine. The same goes for the Russian mercs, they are the ones in charge of security inside the well where the big sub is being held. *That* is your job, understood?"

"Yes, sir."

Put in those terms it made sense, of course. Although the operation had to be much bigger than Admiral Fullerton himself, with all his importance for being who he was, and Yuri Pavenko as well; behind them, I reflected, had to be a world-wide and resourceful organization, perhaps a government, or more than one. A nuclear submarine is not easily bought by anyone.

"I must be honest with you, Pat, this thing is getting complicated," he said, frowning and falling silent again. The degree of apprehension I experienced increased; quite frankly, his attitude was beginning to worry me. "There are other elements at play here. First detail: The new Pavenko henchmen guarding the underwater shipyard may turn out to be no such thing."

"Turn out to be what, sir, mercenaries, or Russians?" I inquired sarcastically, but he surprised me by nodding his head.

"Mercenaries. How did you know? It must be the Scotch; it seems to fire up your brain cells."

"I know *nothing*, Colonel. Or rather, the only thing I know is that, with you, one *never* knows. Just took a wild guess."

He grinned and sipped his Scotch; I did the same. "I hate to be so predictable, Pat, but anyway, I'm afraid those two *boyeviks* are really working for Russia's GRU** and they're coming for Pavenko. I don't have any proof of that, yet, but I can feel it in my gut."

"I understand that the services of the new Russian Federation are collaborating with the OCF in operations against the Russian Mafia, right? All you gotta do is pick up a phone and dial the Moscow Bureau for more information on the case."

"Absolutely not," he interposed sharply. "That's precisely the one thing I *shouldn't* do! It would be a disaster. Think about it."

I did and concluded that perhaps he was right.

"I can't allow them to lay their hands on Yuri now, Pat, not at this critical time for us; I know those two are here to kill him."

"If they intend to do so, they would have done it already, sir, don't you think?"

"Negative. They won't punch his ticket until they know for sure what's going on here; they'll wait for the right moment and if they don't find out anything worth their trouble just by sticking close to him, they'll torture the bastard, or his daughter, and kill them later... Can you imagine the scandal that will break out if Moscow ever learns that Pavenko is our informant?"

"*Your* informant, sir. If it were up to me, that son of a bitch would already be feeding the worms six feet under the ground. And the girl too, mind you, the she-devil almost got me in Cali!"

"You say that because you are not taking into account the big picture, but thanks to Yuri and the deal we have with him, I was able to find out who really is the unknown man who posed as a CIA mole in the Middle East and who, according to Jessica and *you*, stole the briefcase with the money I got you from Mr. Feldman to hook Pavenko."

"You are referring to Commander Ahmed, naturally."

"Naturally!" He mimicked, looking me straight in the eye.

"We already knew who this individual is, Colonel," I interceded, beginning to grow impatient, "a NOC from the CIA..."

"Have you heard of the Islamic Sword?" He stopped me, and now I fully recognized that this project of his, which had begun at a harmless dinner in Washington

D.C., was ballooning more and more, and that, perhaps, in the end it would turn out to be too big for a single operator. Even if he was a hard veteran of the Cold War; like yours truly.

I downed the last of my Scotch and motioned for him to pour me another. As the Colonel rushed to do so, I lit another ciggy. Jessica's absence was beginning to irritate me. Having seen her briefly at headquarters had given me hope that everything would soon be back to normal. Now I was no longer sure.

"Islamic Sword," I muttered, "sounds like jihad to me."

"That's where all this is going," he said. "It is an extremist group that, according to General Cedeño, is based on the periphery of the Colombian/Venezuelan border... Now, there's another development that I must brief you on, because you're going to have to deal with it sooner or later."

"Another development, sir?"

"You do remember General Cedeño, don't you?" He pressed me.

"Yes, sir; the great chieftain of the Colombian Search Bloc. No need to refresh my memory, I remember the gent all right; what about him?

This time his eyes looked down. "Again, all this is very complicated, Pat," he said frowning, and once more my degree of apprehension increased as I caught his gesture, "and I don't want to make a false move. I've already told you that there are other players in the arena...."

"That's right, the Russian mercs; you really think they are GRU people operating undercover?"

He pursed his lips and narrowed his Eskimo dog's eyes. "Very possible. Either way, you will have to get rid of them. If they're Russian operators and they're coming for Pavenko, take them out. And if they're just *Grupa Vagnera* people tasked with protecting the facility, do the same. Are we clear on that, Delta?"

"Yes, sir."

But that wasn't all, there was something else — I could sense it.

However, we were forced to suspend the talk because, just at that instant, a loud knock sounded on the door; someone on the other side seemed bent on breaking it down.

*Refer to the third volume in the series, entitled *One Deadly Souk* (*Author's Note*).
**Russian language acronym for *Glavnoye Razvedovatelnoye Upravlenie*, translated into English as "Army Military Intelligence Directorate" (*Author's Note*).

Chapter 3

THE RESTLESS LIONESS

"**D**amn it..." hissed the Colonel gnashing his teeth while biting the mouthpiece of his briarwood pipe.

"Are we expecting someone, sir?" I inquired while deluding myself to believe that, perhaps, whoever was knocking on the door was my partner, Jessica. But the indiscreet way they had done it indicated otherwise.

For all the answers I saw him scrutinize his wristwatch and grumble. My chief left his seat with un-suspected agility for a man his age and headed for the door, which indicated to me that someone else had indeed been invited to our meeting. The person who entered our room did so with the airs of a tropical storm, carrying in its wake a strong scent of feminine perfume. It smelled good, I won't deny it, but I found the aroma somewhat disturbing under the circumstances. We had gathered there — at least to the best of my knowledge — for professional reasons.

The girl who introduced herself was quite a character, and certainly not who I had imagined, although she was not a total stranger either. The newcomer was a Latin woman, quite tallish for the average of her race, with a curvaceous figure, faint cinnamon-colored skin, and long black hair of silky texture. Her movements were dynamic, elastic, and denoted exasperation. The high degree of tension she was under forced her to take a couple of deep breaths, and the tinted glasses she was wearing seemed to be the only barrier that prevented old Berkowitz from burning under her fierce gaze. I am not exaggerating if I tell you that the situation, far from worrying me, seemed amusing. It's not every day that one can watch the great Marlon Berkowitz being put in his place, you know....

The girl approached him fragrantly, without noticing me. She planted herself in front of my boss and crossed her arms in a gesture of frank defiance.

"Listen to me, Colonel Berkowitz, and listen well!" hissed the restless lioness.

"The next time you decide to employ my services, don't make me wait... Or you'll have to find somebody else!"

Although she and her girls from the Triple K group had been of great help to us during the Caribbean operation, I never imagined that Karina Reyes would ever come to work directly with me.

After my boss briefed her on the aspects of the operation that concerned her, the Colonel got us an SUV and we drove in a hostile silence to the nearest railroad station located in the municipality of Palmira, named *Ferrocarril del Pacífico* — that's Pacific Railroad to you. Karina showed clear signs of still being grumpy and the reason for her displeasure, she later disclosed, was very similar to mine. From the beginning, neither of us looked favorably upon the whimsical rigging to which the Colonel subjected us.

As the vehicle crossed the city, with the girl at the wheel, I rewound my memory to the last scene I had lived in the Colonel's room, at Las Mercedes; it is still vividly engraved in my mind.

"Relax, Miss Reyes," my boss had told her in that poised and dour tone he always uses when it is his turn to neutralize a temperamental crisis. He indicated a vacant sofa and added. "Please, take a seat."

It was then that she became aware of my presence for the first time, a fact that clearly disturbed her. At the sight of me she emitted a wince of protest, but in the end the Latin lioness opted to sit down.

"This gentleman," the Colonel continued, pointing at me, "is Agent Delta. I believe you two already know each other; you coincided briefly in the Aruba operation; do you remember him?"

"Why, yes," she answered, "I had to pull his nuts out of the fire!"

That exclamation of hers, although very true, did not please me at all. The reason for my reaction was the tone of contemptuous superiority with which she articulated the phrase.

"Yeah, I remember her too," I hastened to say, before the Colonel asked me.

"Very well then, since you're both already acquainted," my boss turned to Karina and continued, "let's move on. The mission I'm going to assign you entails two facets, Miss Reyes: the physical elimination of two men who oversee security, a phase that Delta will be taking care of, and the blowing up of the submarine they're guarding. That, Miss Reyes, will be up to you."

We looked at each other without commenting. It was obvious that Karina was assessing me, and I was curious to know how high or low I measured by her standards. For my part, I continued to think that pairing me with this gorgeous Latin lioness — despite her being such a lovely creature — had not been a smart move by my chief, knowing, as he damned well knew, that I have always been a lone wolf. But the gesture should not have surprised me because never, as far as I can remember, did my likes or dislikes mean much to him. He was a dogmatic gent and very jealous of his authority; no one questioned his decisions. In that respect he was very much like Jessica.

After the Land Rover was loaded on board one of the freight cars, we went to the terminal to validate our tickets and half an hour later we were installed in one of the wagons. The locomotive blew a whistle, and we began to leave the railway station behind. Charged with a certain nostalgia, my eyes wandered to the outside of the terminal. Traveling by train is something that has always fascinated me since I was a child, and Denver, my hometown, is home to one of the most legendary and archaic rail terminals in the entire United States: the Union Station, steeped in history, whose origins date back to the times of the Wild West, from its baroque building, built in 1868, to its modern version shopping mall-style with bars and restaurants that cater to various railroad lines. The Rio Grande Zephyr, for instance, although it ceased operations in 1983 to be replaced by the Denver Ski Train Company, which continued to operate until the winter of 2009 and then by the California Zephyr, which came last when the railroad giant AMTRAK swallowed up the independent lines.

"So, we meet again, Delta," spoke Karina suddenly, without turning to look at me, while the monotonous rolling of the heavy metal wheels over the rails served as background to her words. "What happened to that blonde you were teamed up with in Aruba? You don't work together anymore? I could have sworn you kind of liked each other... Karmen never realized the tall white bitch was no lesbian, the *güerita** just played her, but I guess she never took my partner seriously. Am I wrong?"

I didn't answer that, nor did I turn to look at her closely as her beauty warranted, although I was already beginning to burn with the desire to do so. But her shrewd comment about the waggish incident between a blonde-haired Jessica and the Triple K group's gay operator back in Aruba, kind of soured my mood.

"Oh boy," said Karina at last and let out a sigh, "he got his tongue eaten out by mice! I hope you don't turn out to be one of those officious Gringos who look down their noses at Latinos."

"You are Colombian, aren't you?"

"What makes you think that?" she spat out, almost violently.

"I understand that your relationship with my boss comes through General Cedeño, and he is Colombian... that's my reason."

"Well, you are badly mistaken, *señor güero*; I have Mexican blood in my veins, and it comes out. Don't get confused."

And believe me when I tell you that if I laughed at my boss before, when the Colonel confronted this Latin lioness in his room at Las Mercedes, I was sure that the old fox was having the last laugh at my expense, by just imagining how I would be dealing with this fiery Aztec goddess, as magnificent as she was imperious.

Güero, güerito (masculine) or *güera, güerita* (feminine) is the Mexican slang to define a person with a fair complexion (*Author's Note*).

Chapter 4

GETTING TO KNOW YOUR ALLIES

At first, the idea of traveling by train and road seemed to me to be a big waste of time, when it was possible to cover the same distance quicker by plane. But little by little I began to grasp the logic behind the Colonel's decision. The old fox was giving us time to mingle.

Our destination was the Atlantic coast — well, Barranquilla, to be exact. When the train could not continue due to the absence of rails, we dismounted, climbed aboard the SUV and headed down a long road called Route 45. First, we went through Pereira; then we crossed Puerto Boyacá, followed by Barrancabermeja, San Alberto and Agua Chica. We arrived in Cienega and there, just before reaching Santa Marta, we turned west and did not stop until we entered Barranquilla. The first thing you notice when you get there, naturally, is that it's a port city as beautiful and lively as few others in the southern cone of the American continent. Which made sense, of course, given the characteristics of our mission.

Miss Reyes, who claimed to know the area well, insisted that we stay at a place named El Rodadero, one of the most popular beach resorts in the region, where, according to the good people at the Culture & Tourism Bureau, you can swim with dolphins. I didn't think it was a bad idea, you know, in such a crowded place it's difficult to attract attention and with a little luck and tact we could pass for simple tourists. Sometime later, once already lodged at El Rodadero, where we settled in a single room as husband and wife, I poured myself a drink from the bar cabinet and plopped down on one end of the kidney-shaped sofa that rested on the thick carpet, next to the terrace overlooking the Atlantic Ocean. Karina sat at the other end of the comfortable piece of furniture, with an electronic tablet resting on her knees, the gadget contained the two Russian mercenaries' files and all the information my boss kept sending to layer the mission.

"How do you feel?" I heard her mumble.

"What exactly do you mean?" I answered her question with another.

"How is your morale, *güero*, what else could it be? Aren't you a bit concerned? I've been going over the files of those two characters, the ones in charge of shipyard security. They're dangerous, you know, I'm sure your chief must have warned you."

"Are you trying to teach grandma how to suck an egg?" I hissed.

"Grandma? Suck eggs? What the hell are you talking about?"

The crankiness with which she snapped at me made me look into her eyes; she appeared confused. Then I realized that the Spanish translation of that old Gringo aphorism was not entirely understandable for a person born and raised in another country. Don't teach your grandmother how to suck an egg, in my native language, is equivalent to *don't teach a professional how to do his job*. But I wasn't in the mood to explain this to her.

"Never mind, Miss Reyes," I growled.

"You really need to take them seriously, Delta. I'm only pointing it out because you haven't even deigned to scan their files once throughout the entire journey…" she paused meaningfully before adding, "you should stop staring at my legs and put your mind where it should be, *your* targets."

Oh, she was right about that. With the number of years I've spent in the trade one sometimes relies too much on experience and the set of skills acquired over time, neglecting to pay due attention to the written details. The ones that really count. But admiring her legs seduced me much more than being impressed by the Russians' files. If the Colonel says they were *good*, then they were good and that was it; no further briefing was needed. However, I neither added nor subtracted anything from what the operator of the Triple K Group was saying; I just looked her in the eye, nodded my head, and continued to silently admire her lower limbs. Hers was a body worthy of a goddess from the ancient Greece.

"Did you hear me, *güero*? Or are you playing possum?"

"Calm down, sister, there's no reason to take things so personally," I growled between my teeth, "I already know what there is to know about those guys, believe me. Even down to the fact that they once belonged to the elite troops of the Soviet Navy. Satisfied?"

"Hell, no! I *insist* that you should familiarize yourself with their files. Oh, and don't call me sister, I am not. I like my name very much; use it!" She paused during which her gaze rammed into mine, but she immediately softened her tone and spoke… "I'm sorry, Delta. I know I'm being rude to you, but it's just that I'm uncomfortable working in pairs with new people…, and to top it off *your* boss… Well, you know him better than me, he's infuriating at times!"

Her comment about the Colonel took me by surprise.

"Trust me, I understand," I hastened to say, now that for the first time she was holding out an olive branch to me and, besides, we had converged on a common point; that my boss was exasperating was something I shared with her one hundred percent. "I'm aware that the Colonel is not an easy man to deal with. I didn't know that you two knew each other from way back. It was my understanding that your liaison with the Quadrille was through General Cedeño."

"Partly so, but I have done a few minor assignments for Col. Berkowitz in the past, sometimes teamed up with Karmen and Kayla; sometimes by myself, as on this occasion.

"You must be very good, then; I first knew you as a sniper and now it turns out you're also an explosives expert, right?"

"I'm good," she reaffirmed haughtily raising her head and displaying her full sovereign bust, swollen now by exaggerated Mexican pride, "don't doubt it, *güero*. I trained with your Green Berets in Panama, when the School of the Americas operated in that zone under the Southern Command."

"I don't belittle you, Miss Reyes. Relax. The Colonel has used you before, which I know for a fact; now he has called on you again and that speaks highly of your integrity and your skills."

To tell the truth, I was not so sure that this was the real motive for her participation in this operation. My boss, being so Machiavellian as the old fox is, could have ulterior motives that had little or nothing to do with Miss Reyes' skills, I told myself, though I did not mention it. A little voice inside me forewarned me about that possibility, because working on my superior's personal projects is something that was always done under a sacrosanct rule: *Cover your tracks and watch your back*. And, for that, you always need a fall guy — or a fall gal.

"All right, I believe you. But it doesn't stop worrying me the way you're underestimating that pair of killers... Please, understand that with them hanging around the shipyard, my job becomes more complicated. Those sons of bitches are as dangerous as a pair of tigers."

"I know that." I spat out grudgingly. "I just don't see why we should worry at the moment; let us relax a little, okay; it helps the body prepare for action."

She drew a long breath. "You may be right, Delta," she conceded, a moment before her expressive eyes followed the trajectory of my gaze to her legs. "You really are enjoying yourself, aren't you?"

"What?" I asked, making the face of a kid caught red-handed with his hand inside the cookie jar. "C'mon, give me a break!"

"Don't act so innocent, *güero*, you haven't stopped staring at my legs since we got on the train!"

"Oh, just shut your trap for a few minutes, will you!" I burst into feigned anger, though I was rejoicing inside. "I hate blabbermouths, and *you* cluck more than a broody hen!"

To my surprise, my feigned bitterness, far from annoying her, seemed to amuse her. Throwing her head back, Karina let out a laugh so stentorian and crystalline that it rubbed off on me.

While my new partner and I endeavored to find the best way to work as a team on our present assignment, the Colonel was arriving in Barranquilla by his own means. One of the rumors concerning my chief among the members of the Quadrille — I mean our old outfit, the one from the Cold War era — was that the old man was a drag in the theater of operations, and that he was incapable of carrying his own weight. Well, it's normal to think that of any boss and in this case even more so, because the kind of mental profile of those who deal in the clandestine ops business tends to be skeptical by nature and — to a certain degree — contemptuous of all those around. Even old Tilson commented behind his back, of course, that if the Colonel was ever snatched from his desk, a battalion of Marines would be required to rescue him... An exaggeration, to be sure, but many of my colleagues at the time shared his opinion. Except Agent Landon, who had been with the Colonel in Vietnam when Marlon Berkowitz was still active with the Special Forces and not just planning operations behind a desk but carrying them out in the field as well with a handful of men. And I, because I sensed it from the very first day I laid eyes on him. In this turn of events, one learns to discern the wolves from the dogs, and Col. Marlon Berkowitz — mind you — was a ferocious wolf in every sense of the word.

That very same day, a few hours before Miss Reyes and I checked in at the El Rodadero resort, the Colonel arrived on a commercial flight with Avianca Airlines that touched down at the Ernesto Cortissoz International Airport in the city of Barranquilla. In fact, my boss did not come out of the plane alone, he was pushing a wheelchair in which he carried a Black man several years older than himself, probably in his seventies, with short kinky hair dotted with gray spots. The man bore a remarkable resemblance to actor Morgan Freeman, but his real name was Bill Johnson and Bill was always the official armorer of the Quadrille. The wheelchair he rode in was a work of art, carefully designed and assembled by himself at his workshop in the Special Effects Department he ran altogether with the Armory.

When I heard about it, I could not help but wonder how it was possible that Bill the Armorer had allowed himself to be dragged into one of my boss's personal projects and the only motive I came up with was that the man was dying of boredom in his post-retirement period and that staying within the circle of CI5's covert ops was the only way to ease the boredom and still feel alive... Alive and useful to his country. Like Karina and I, both men took up a suite at El Rodadero, but I did not find out about it until a little later.

However, my chief and Bill were not the only ones; soon after Nina and Yuri showed up.

Chapter 5

AN UNEXPECTED BRUSH

As soon as my chief and his companion occupied a room with the same comforts as ours, Bill Johnson abandoned the wheelchair and rolled it into the bedroom. The Colonel followed in his footsteps and closed the curtains on the windows overlooking the sea, then turned on the lights and watched as Johnson took the chair apart and carefully placed each piece on the bed. Since it had been Bill himself who had designed, built and assembled it in his Special Effects workshop at CI5 headquarters, he had engineered it so that the assembly and disassembly work did not require the use of tools. The process was reduced to simple twisting and unscrewing of the interconnected parts.

"It was an excellent idea to fill all those tubes with plastique and use a medicinal pillbox to carry the mini grenades." Said my boss, referring to the tiny pill-shaped pickles and the plastic explosive paste that is soft and can be molded by hand, like plasticine. The version they were using is called C-4, an explosive element that, along with Semtex, is considered a modern derivative of the original gelignite invented by one Alfred Nobel in the late 19th century.

Johnson only grunted at the comment and once he had the plastic pillbox containing the grenade capsules and all the C-4 paste out of the tubes that formed the skeleton of the chair, he cut it with a folding knife without removing it from its cellophane wrapping to form small bars, as if they were ingots. From one of the suitcases that made up the luggage, Bill extracted what at first glance looked like a medium-sized gift box and opened it. From inside he took out a roll of waxed paper, with which he began to cover the C-4 bars he had already cut.

"There you go," spoke up the Armorer once he had wrapped the last of the poles and was arranging them all on the mattress.

The Colonel nodded approvingly and handed him one of the larger suitcases they had brought with them as part of the luggage. Bill took the suitcase and placed it on the bed, undid the locks and began to place everything neatly inside. Just then there were three knocks on the door in rapid succession.

Johnson stopped his chores, the Colonel checked his wristwatch and waited tensely, exactly two seconds elapsed before they knocked again. This time it was two knocks only but spaced apart.

"It must be Cedeño," murmured my boss and hurried to open the door. When he did, the silhouettes of two men in civilian clothes appeared on the lintel, cut out against the light. One of them, in fact, belonged to General Bartolo Cedeño of the Colombian Search Bloc and the other to his assistant. Someone with whom my chief and I had previously collaborated: *Señor* César Zambrano Lora*.

It was only a few hours that Karina and I spent resting from the trip — five or six, if I remember correctly. After taking a cold shower to clear my head and ordering something to eat from room service over the phone, I dressed in a pair of faded and battered denim shorts that I got from my travel backpack, a pair of canvas flat-soled tennis shoes and a mustard-colored Polo shirt. I didn't bother to wear socks because this was a tropical beach environment anyway; hardly anyone here wore them. I also grabbed a pair of sunglasses to round out my vacationer image, and taking advantage of the fact that Karina was still engaged in the process of contacting her people in the area via Internet, I set out to check on our Land Rover in its assigned parking space. I wanted to make sure it was still intact, right where we had left it. Local crime in places such as this one, where there is a big tourist boom, is usually rampant and I was worried that our Jeep would be stolen because it was such an exotic and expensive vehicle.

"Hey," I told her before living the room, "I'm going to check on our transport, be back soon."

"Suit yourself, *güero*," was her reply, which she articulated sort of absently as her swift fingers typed fluently, never taking her eyes off her tablet's screen.

Closing the door behind me, I went down to the lobby and, on the way to the main doors, I stopped briefly at the reception counter to ask if there were any messages waiting for us. This was not the case, so I thanked the receptionist and resumed my walk.

Our weapons and equipment for this operation were hidden in the cargo bay of the SUV. There were two German-made Heckler & Koch Model MP5 submachine guns, with their corresponding magazines capable of holding up to thirty Parabellum 9x19 millimeter caliber cartridges. There was a pair of American-made pistols, both twins, of the Smith & Wesson brand, model SW22 Victory. Just like the SMGs, both were equipped with noise suppressors and several ammo clips, the cartridges they fired were .22LR in caliber. Like the MP5s, these were very reliable weapons, especially for close-range work: accurate, light and quiet. All wrapped in black canvas bags with waterproof lining.

I arrived next to the Jeep; took the key fob out of a pocket and deactivated the alarm before opening the trunk door. I inspected the cargo bay carefully and made sure that the things that really mattered to us were still intact in their place. I also checked inside the cabin, there were no hidden microphones; then I got out and lifted the hood just in case and made sure no one had been fiddling with the distributor wires nor the spark plugs or the brake fluid reservoir cap; the hydraulic lines were undamaged; they hadn't been cut. Nor had a bomb been planted there. Everything seemed to be in proper order, but when I lowered the hood again, I felt a strange vibration behind me and suddenly I sensed there was someone lurking around. I am not a superstitious man; I only believe in God and the devil. But that feeling of anxiety that assaulted me had nothing to do with the Almighty, quite the contrary, and the only time I remember having experienced something similar before in my entire life had been precisely here, in Colombia, although not in a seaside resort on the Atlantic coast but in a suburb of Santiago de Cali, in a discotheque in Juanchito. There is no better phrase to describe it than "perceiving the shadow of evil."

As I suddenly turned around, the hairs on the back of my neck stood up like the spikes of a porcupine, although I could see no one else in the surrounding area; however, that evil feeling of being spied on did not dissipate. I swallowed dryly and stood very still, sharpening my hearing as much as possible. I felt the faint brush of footsteps on the asphalt, so I spun again and this time I did catch a glimpse of the blowing wisps of a straight black mane — a woman's hair, judging by the length and its shape — disappearing behind a nearby column. *Karina...?* I remember thinking. Perhaps she'd followed me here with the purpose of watching me at work, but I immediately dismissed that possibility because the owner of that furtive head of hair finally stepped out in the clear, and soon I had a beautiful woman standing right in front of me. The first thing I noticed was that she was a lot younger than my partner in crime in this operation; the second thing, that she was aiming a compact semi-auto straight at my face.

Nina the Gunslinger!

"Stand still, *Amerikanskiy*!" she hissed in an almost imperceptible tone, and I noticed that her pulse did not waver; the pistol she was aiming at me was rock-steady between her fingers.

Her unexpected appearance stunned me for a moment. Despite her adorable nymph-like appearance brimming in youth, Nina Tetriak was one of the best pros in the killing business I'd faced in recent times after my return to the Quadrille. Knowing this prompted me to separate my hands from my body and show her my empty palms so that she could see I was not armed. We had met once before, and I was aware of how accurate her fiendish aim could be; but my experience told me that, if she'd really been sent to eliminate me, she'd already had plenty of time to do so.

"Easy now, you infernal creature..." I hissed, looking straight into her eyes. They were dead eyes, very large and as unfathomably black as a pit of crude oil, but glazed and impenetrable like those of a dangerous reptile, devoid of all expression, the eyes of a professional assassin. "Don't go do anything you'll regret," I told her. "I don't know if you're aware of it, Nina, but we're partners with your sugar daddy. Yuri must have told you."

She didn't respond to this, just approached me very cautiously keeping her armed hand close to her side, to dishearten any attempt to disarm her with a kick from me; well, I already said she was a pro. The girl slipped her other hand into her cleavage and held it out to me. I could see that it held a folded piece of paper.

"Take this, *Amerikanskiy*," Nina said quietly, "it's a message."

I reached out my right hand and grabbed the piece of paper she handed me. I only took my eyes off her figure for a fraction of a second, but that was enough for her to vanish. I never saw or heard her again; it was a ghostly disappearance. Then I turned because I immediately perceived other footsteps, but these were the firm and determined footsteps of someone who had no reason to hide. Instinctively, I slipped the piece of paper into a pocket and spotted the familiar figure of a man emerge from behind one of the concrete columns. My mind still retained his vivid image. The gent that walked toward the SUV was carrying a suitcase in his hand.

"Cesar," I gasped in surprise, "what the hell are *you* doing here!"

*Refer to the third volume in the series, entitled *One Deadly Souk* (*Author's Note*).

THE HIDDEN GROTTO

Part Two

Chapter 6

A MESSAGE FROM BEYOND

"*Hola*, Mr. Coonan," uttered General Cedeño's aid-de-camp as he greeted me in his native tongue, grinning at my astonishment, "didn't your chief tell you that we would be operating together on this one too?"

Before answering the question with which he had answered mine, I searched his gaze for traces of having noticed the exchange that had taken place just seconds before between Nina and yours truly but found no hint of it. Keeping my eyes fixed on his, I drew a long breath. At least the man hadn't called me "Agent Coonan" out loud, though I would have preferred if he had left my last name out. A simple *how are you, friend* was more than enough, wasn't it?

But these gentlemen from the interior of the country, the non-coastal ones, I mean, as was the case of Mr. Zambrano Lora, are soft-spoken and rigorously correct in their speech — even the big drug lords of Colombia when they are natives of the Andean lands behave that way, with lots of class, all properly said and correctly expressed, which does not prevent them from carving a Colombian necktie at knife point on your throat, when the occasion arises. And friend Cesar was a paradigm of the classic *cachaco**: elegant, restrained, well educated; without any of this inhibiting him from taking out that heavy semi-auto that he used to carry under the armpit and shoot you right through the forehead. I then reflected, with the bitterness of someone who has fucked up and admits it, that I had also screwed up first by addressing him by his first name. But having to deal so unexpectedly with a she-devil like Nina, and on top of that, with the surprise of seeing him suddenly materialize, it was upsetting; that's the truth.

What can I say, you know; nobody's perfect.

Cesar arrived at my side and handed me the suitcase he was carrying. He didn't say what it was, he didn't even give me a hint, he just glanced sideways at the Land Rover's luggage rack and his gesture was more eloquent than a political candidate's speech. The meaning was clear to me: What he was handing me was part of our arsenal. I took the suitcase with a nod of my head and put it away along with the weapons. I didn't make the mistake of asking him about the contents, it must have been the explosive required to blow up Fullerton's sub, since it was the only thing we were missing and probably a couple of other novelties like those ingenious gadgets that Bill the Armorer prepares for us from time to time. I would have time to check it all out, I told myself, before we set out on our river journey.

"Shall we, uh, have a cup of coffee?" the little man asked softly, "I'm buying."

I glanced at my Rolex wristwatch, the *Submariner* model, if it matters. "Sure," I told him. "As long as we don't have to move away from the area. I don't want to leave my wife alone for too long."

The last sentence I said raising my voice a little, so that everyone could hear me without someone investing their time in spying on us.

We did not walk far, Cesar guided me to a typical rest-aurant of the type that abounds in El Rodadero and ordered two coffees. We took a booth and when we were served the steaming brew, the Colombian agent tasted his and began to talk: "Your chief is staying here, in a room not far from yours, but he does not wish to have direct contact with you in public; there may be other interested parties hanging around, *amigo*. Do I make myself clear?"

"Crystal clear. What about *your* chief?" I asked. "Is the General in town?

Cesar nodded his head. "At this very moment he is meeting with your boss and one other gentleman. A very tall and very serious Negro..."

"Does he look like actor Morgan Freeman?" I interrupted him.

"How did you know?" He grinned and I realized it was one of those questions you ask without expecting an answer.

"I know the gent," I stated, clicking my tongue. "I bet he was the one who delivered that lump for me."

"You know him well then." Cesar widened his grin. "He did."

I took a sip of the coffee, which was delicious, and lit a cancer stick.

"Cigarette?" I inquired, showing him the pack and lighter.

"No, thank you. When do you plan to leave?"

"As soon as I get back to the room and we finalize the details of our little river trip, my wife is taking care of that now. We rested enough to continue the march and if what you have given me is what we were missing, well, let's just say that I don't see a valid reason to hang around."

"I see," he showed me two fingers, before adding, "a couple of things, Mr. Coonan. In the suitcase you will find a satellite phone."

Another one? I thought, I already had one that Bill had given me, in Miami, before traveling to Colombia. However, I said nothing.

"There are two numbers programmed in speed dial mode. If you press the first digit on the digital board, it will connect you to a direct and secure line with your chief. If you press the second digit, you will be calling me and my chief. Please use it as you see fit, from now until the end of your fluvial excursion we will remain at your service, but don't let that gizmo fall into enemy hands, *comprende?* They could track our location with it. Destroy it first before you allow it to be confiscated against your will. Orders from your chief. You copy?"

"Duly noted, Cesar. What's the second thing?"

"There are other gadgets included in your arsenal that serve different purposes, when you talk to your chief ask him about them. That's all I have for you now. If you should ever need me, remember, use that number."

"Great. *Gracias, amigo.*"

"You are welcome. Anything to report? Any message for your employer?"

"Not particularly. Just tell him that so far everything is going smoothly and that I'll be in touch with him soon. I can't give you an exact time, because I don't know, although I hope to be able to contact him before the end of today. That's all, Cesar."

"I'll let him know. Good luck to you and, as you know, we are at your service."

I nodded and smiled. After all, I can't say I disliked the guy.

"My regards to your beautiful *señora*," he winked at me, "enjoy the excursion and *vayan con Dios.*"

"Let's hope so, *amigo. Muchas gracias.*"

When I returned to our room, I found Karina locked in the bathroom, so I took the opportunity to extract from my pocket the folded paper the Russian assassin had handed me in the hotel parking lot. I unfolded it and read the note that someone — I assumed Yuri — was sending me. The missive was written in Cyrillic, it read as follows: *andreikodina.gru.aktivnyy*. The first thing that came to my mind was to ask what the hell is this? After looking at it more closely I began to think that it could be an e-mail or a website of sorts, if I added *.org* at the end; or *.com*. It didn't turn out to be that. With the piece of paper in hand I stepped onto the balcony with the intention of burning it using my lighter, or the same red tip of the ciggy I lit on the terrace, after returning to study the message once more. I stopped to read it aloud and then it dawned on me that *andreikodina* was Andrei Kodina, a Russian name and surname that suddenly began to sound familiar and, as I repeated it several times, led me to think of an Andrei Kodina I had heard of more than fifteen years ago and who, in some darned way that I could not quite evoke, was linked to old Yuri Pavenko's past and the late Soviet KGB. Mm...

Therefore: *Andrei Kodina is an active member of the GRU.*

"Eureka!" I mumbled to myself. But I immediately understood that, although I had managed to decipher the message, I still didn't grasp its relation to the mission. I would have to check with my boss, maybe he could shed some light on the mystery. But what struck me most was that to me the name Andrei Kodina, regardless of the past link to my first caper with the Quadrille** still sounded newly familiar.

Where the hell have I heard this name before? I thought.

Just at that instant the flushing of the toilet reached

my ears and the bathroom door opened as Karina stepped back into the room. She spotted me smoking on the balcony, smiled and went to sit on her corner of the kidney-shaped leather sofa. She picked up the tablet, set it on her knees and began to type. I finished smoking my cigarette and burned the piece of paper carrying Yuri's message and the scribbles I had added myself in the process of deciphering it. I stomped on the ashes and scattered them in the wind. Then I returned to the living room, walked to the bar cabinet, poured two glasses of the whiskey we had in reserve and took one to the girl.

She took the container from my hand, looked at it with some disdain and briefly sniffed its contents. "Scotch," she stated. "I'm not really that excited about it, but in the absence of vodka or tequila..."

I grinned at the hint and went to sit at the other end of the couch, where I settled in with my own glass in hand and again pinned my eyes to her lower extremities. Her thighs were a delight, there's no denying it, and that smooth skin of hers of a slight caramel tone incited me to caress it. Putting aside all my prejudices, I focused on sipping my Scotch and undressing her with my sight.

"All done, *güero*; we'll use a fisherman from the area who goes by the nickname Coco; he just agreed to transport us to the theater of operations."

"Splendid," I said.

Ipso facto she stood up with the tablet in one hand and the drink in the other and walked to my side of the sofa, where she flexed her knees and planted her lovely derriere on the space next to me. Then Karina placed the electronic gadget on my lap. I did not overlook that, with the change in position, the skin of her thighs now brushed against mine.

"Here, let me show you something; see that spot there? That's the area where our target is located. These are the satellite images just transmitted to us by the Colonel. What you're looking at is the shipyard we're going to visit at the bottom of the grotto. Apparently, it is an abandoned site, but the spies that General Cedeño has moved into the area have reported that the cavern is very wide and deep, and the submarine, as the diagram shows, is submerged in it to keep it from being discovered should any unwelcome visitors suddenly show up... You know, people like us." She finished with a malicious wink.

"Which means that the work crew they're using to dismantle the ship works submerged, right?"

"Correct."

"Wow... how ingenious. That way they minimize the chance of being detected by the satellites," but then again, being aware of it made me reflect that, if there was such a secret shipyard deep inside the grotto and a work crew onsite, it was also likely that Admiral Fullerton and his group of collaborators would be present to supervise the operation. Which added more targets to my list, right? And then I wondered if Col. Berkowitz might not be overestimating my powers. Any way you looked at it, I was not a Marvel-class superhero — or even a DC-class one, for that matter — and the orders he'd given me were beginning to seem like too much for a single eliminator. Even if the chosen operative was Agent Delta, I reflected with fateful sarcasm. But then I remembered my brief meeting with Cesar and the satellite phone the little man had given me and, believe it or not, I felt better, calmer. Besides, Karina had just mentioned that General Cedeño had people deployed in the region with their eyes on the shipyard hidden in the underwater cave, and the Search Bloc team commandos probably belonged to a very well-armed Special Reconnaissance Group, positioned there to come to my aid, if I required it.... I grinned.

Yeah, when you took this into consideration, my odds were improving, weren't they?

"Anything else, Miss Reyes?" I asked.

"Your chief also sent us the schematics for the sub, it's one of the Ohio-class. I calculate that the Russian mercs must be passing for onsite workers. The management must be local, so as not to attract attention."

Which was only logical, but at the mention of the Russian mercenaries I realized that, although my boss suspected that they were GRU assassins operating incognito, neither of them — if I was well informed — was named Andrei Kodina, of that I was sure; but even so the doubt made its way into my head, because at this point I still could not place the importance of said name... *Andrei Kodina, hum...* Something was beginning to tell me that this Kodina character was a relevant piece in the matter, more important for the solution of the problem than any forgetful imbecile (like yours truly here) could suspect. Otherwise, Yuri would never have sent his girl to run the risk of approaching me with the message. He was a suspicious bastard both by nature and profession, but I could understand his preference to approach me rather than my chief, whom he probably feared a lot more. After all, I had had a chance to eliminate him in the past and had not yet done so. That, in a way, had established a precedent; a sort of psychological bond, even if it was a vague one.

Yuri and Patrick, I mused, *two friendly adversaries.*

"Now that you mention them," I said, "it's about time for me to look up their files before I set out to deal with them. Do you have them handy?"

"Yep. Thought you'd never ask."

"Thanks. One question, Miss Reyes: How do you propose we do this?"

She thought hard for a few seconds before answering:

"Well, it seems to me the best way will be to sneak in from underneath. Coco is a very resourceful feller, and he can infiltrate us by amphibious means, which in my opinion is ideal in this case. He owns a homemade midget sub that we can use to reach the grotto. There must be some sort of trapdoor in the rocks surrounding it, don't you think? It's the only way they could get that monster sub inside that cave where the shipyard has been built."

"I agree. There must be some giant underwater hatch, or a large opening through which, once disassembled, they can move the parts out of the grotto and back into the river. I mean, if that's what they're doing."

"Indeed." She made a quick mental calculation and said: "There are only three charges to place, Delta. Stern, turret and propeller, I think that will do the job. What about you, how do you plan to neutralize the Russies?"

"To be honest, I don't know yet," I said, "and I won't make any guesses until I have a chance to study the activity on the spot and get the pulse of it; I know we have the schematics and all that, but I am somewhat old-fashioned in this respect and prefer to reconnoiter the terrain myself so I can form a true-to-veridical sketch of the situation; I hate to speculate based on plans alone. Sorry, it's just my style. But as for your phase of the mission, everything you've told me seems reasonable. I think the plan will work."

And that was the first time I saw her smile with gusto; all in all, it was falling off the wall that she was a woman who was very jealous of her professional reputation. *Just like Jessica*, I reflected. This competitive modern world, to which I sometimes find it hard to adapt, is full of spoken and challenging females. But what can you do, you know, it's the sign of the times.

While Karina dressed up in a seductive outfit for the

meeting with the boatman and applying the perfect make-up to highlight her beauty, I read the files of the Russies, as she called them. The experience of both operators was quite impressive, but what worried me the most was to confirm that neither of them was named Andrei Kodina. According to the files one was Misha Sokolov, and his partner was Valentin Abramovich. To lighten my mood, I ended up nicknaming them Heckel and Jeckel, like the two talking magpies from the Terrytoons.

Andrei Kodina — if you must know — was their superior.

Before leaving, we went through the entire arsenal once more, which we did separately, opening bag by bag in the cargo bay of the SUV, so that if anything escaped one of us, the other would catch it. Karina was first while I stood guard, smoking a ciggy while leaning against the body of the Land Rover. I felt her moving back and forth on all fours inside the vehicle, sometimes swinging the car's suspension and sometimes not. When she was satisfied, she got out and gave me the thumbs up before taking my place while I went about the business of double-checking everything.

The explosives were in perfect order and were packed together with two boxes of what they call a "pencil detonator" or "timing pencil," which is nothing more than a timing fuse that connects to a short safety fuse. They are approximately the same size and shape as a pencil, hence the origin of their name. Pencil-type detonators are color-coded to indicate their delay time, which can range from ten minutes to twenty-four hours. No. 10 delays are normally packed in a tin of five, all at the same interval, while L delays are packed in a larger tin that includes a composite of different delays adaptable to the features of the operation.

After being activated, a pencil timer runs silently; it does not bubble or make any other noise. But unlike clockwork timers, they only give you approximate time delays. That is, a two-hour pencil might have an accuracy margin of plus or minus five minutes, while the other version offering a six-hour delay might have a margin of plus or minus fifteen minutes. However, the primary virtue of these devices is their diminutive size and light weight — something that, in our current mission, was of vital importance — as well as being quick and easy to use. So, Bill Johnson had supplied us with two boxes of them, one pack of five No. 10 type pencils and another of ten L type pencils mixed, giving us a total of fifteen detonators of different delays; more than enough to do the job with an acceptable margin of error, which was achieved by inserting two delays per charge. If one failed, which sometimes happens, the pair would get the job done.

Returning the detonators and the papered bars of plastic explosive to the suitcase, I took out the satellite phone and powered it on. It was about time I exchanged a few words with the Colonel. I made a mental note to give Karina the other satellite phone, the one Bill Johnson had given me in Miami before flying to Colombia, so we would both have direct access to my chief, in case I would not survive the mission. But before doing so, I checked the rest of the equipment that Bill the Armorer had packed for us. I found what looked like two very peculiar cases shaped like vitamin pillboxes that carried something like pills. They were not cyanide capsules because their casing was made of metal and, therefore, insoluble in human saliva, but I did not rack my brains trying to guess their use; Bill, or the Colonel, would inform me. The rest of the equipment, the weapons and all the paraphernalia of the combat swimmers, were still in perfect order. I put everything back, organizing it just as we had found it.

Finally, I got out of the SUV with the satellite phone in my right and approached Karina. "Everything is in order, Miss Reyes." I said in response to her inquisitive look. "Take this, it's for you," I handed her the phone, "just in case Coco's midget sub's dashboard breaks down or something. You may contact the Colonel through this. They gave me an identical phone with his number saved in its memory. Punch the first digit to reach Col. Berkowitz, and the second if you need to get hold of me. Copy?"

"Roger that."

"Very well, now get behind the wheel and boot the engine. Warm it up while I take care of calling the Colonel and report we are leaving El Rodadero."

"Will do," the girl nodded and entered the cabin.

*In Colombia, the term *cachaco* (pronounced *cash-ah-co* in Spanish) is normally used to refer to a generation of Bogotanos born or influenced by the culture and fashion of the city during the first half of the 20th century and who over time have gradually faded from the capital's scene. They were characterized not only by their elegance and rigor in dress, but also by their dialect (*Author's Note*).

**Refer to the first book in the series, titled *The Quadrille* (*Author's Note*.)

Chapter 7

THE RUSSIAN PUZZLE

We had to get on *Vía 40* and go down to Barranquillita, go past it and take *Carrera 4,* which runs parallel to the river, and then turns off to the east. We kept on driving until we reached the banks of the Magdalena River, not far from the Barranquilla International Terminal Company. Coco was already waiting for us. I didn't miss the lascivious look with which he greeted Karina, something understandable due to the exotic beauty of the voluptuous Mexican that she had purposely groomed for the meeting, but I confess that in some way that I couldn't quite explain her seductive tactics upset me. Some might attribute it to the male ego, although Miss Reyes was still far from being mine, or perhaps it was because, in matters of sex and romance, I'm quite possessive — though I hide it well — and my phallocratic instinct, at the mere fact of desiring her, made me see her as *mine.* Oh, well; the truth is she wasn't.

The fact is that Coco didn't inspire confidence in me and I'm sure he sensed it. Perhaps that's why he kept his distance from yours truly and the entire transaction that required the arrangement was resolved between them two. Karina paid him in advance and the Colombian boatman took us to his boat, which had the name *Sirena* painted on its keel. The vessel was nineteen meters long by eight and a half wide, heavy and slow like a shrimp boat, but under the hull was attached the homemade midget submarine, which made it an essential piece for our underwater caper. It was a metal cylinder twelve meters long by two and a half wide; it was shaped like a torpedo: with a pointed bow, a stern propeller and a fiberglass dome protecting the cockpit. Coco had painted it in different shades of green and blue, replicating the military camouflage pattern. The cargo bay was located at the bow of the cylinder.

Looking at the ingenious device made me suspect that our boatman was not exactly a clean slate, of course; and much less an entity alien to the business of drug trafficking. But if I learned anything from the Colonel in all those years I spent with the Quadrille, it was that the end always justifies the means. If associating ourselves with a small local drug smuggler allowed us to eliminate in one fell swoop a colossal mule for the big cartels and some terrorist groups, capable of transporting tons of weapons, well, what can I say... Do the math and see.

Before Karina and I went into the water, we synchronized our watches with Coco's and split up a pair of transceivers, programmed in advance to the same frequency, in case the need arose to contact him; although, as Miss Reyes explained to me, the deal with the fisherman only covered the outward journey. The return trip — if there was one — would have to be made aboard the midget sub. We would sail it back to the same point on the riverbank where we had met him, in the vicinity of the Barranquilla International Terminal, Co.

After changing into neoprene suits and securing the oxygen tanks on our backs, we put on the rest of the combat swimmer paraphernalia and submerged in the foggy waters of the Magdalena. The skin on my face and hands, which had come into contact with the river water, made me thank God that the rest of my body was covered in rubber. The cold was so sharp that it took my breath away; but that was to be expected, given that this is a muddy, sand-free bottom, where the temperature in its deepest parts always tends to be lower than in the sea of the tropics. Coco began the task of lowering the waterproof bags that contained all our little arsenal, and I felt myself being dragged to the bottom by the weight of my attire. We put everything inside the submarine through the access hatch and Karina helped me check the condition of the equipment once again and stock the packages in the cargo bay. Then we settled into the cabin. Near the bottom, visibility was rather limited, but the midget sub's side lights brightened the ship's contours with faint halos of what looked like liquefied gold, lightening the viscous opacity of the bottom water as they sprinkled their amber light around us.

It was a ghostly journey through a nebulous world, in which only the thin shaft of light projected by the prow of the capsule that carried us and the smallest surrounding lanterns that illuminated the contours of the ship opened a gap of hope. Its yellowish glow highlighted the fauna of the bottom landscape as we passed; the masses of a dull brown that made up the muddy ground; the various types of freshwater fish (carp, mojarras and trout) turned into soft flashes as they moved from east to west, or north to south. I saw some river turtles with very long necks hide their heads as we passed, but what worried me most down there was an encounter with the fearsome boa constrictors and the horrible American crocs — many of which reach six meters in length, almost half the size of our transport. If there was anything to console my phobias, it was that Coco's submarine was well built. Above us we could see the oval spot that was the bottom of the *Sirena*, sailing in a steady course towards our destination. The boat towed us to the agreed point and when we reached it, its engines stopped. Coco activated a mechanism on board the boat and we felt how the sub uncoupled from the mother ship and began a slow descent. Karina activated the propeller motor on the control panel and programmed the GPS. She studied the readings on the dashboard screen for a few seconds and pointed out the target to me, as soon as it became a luminous point on the quadrant; then she connected the autopilot and loaded the coordinates into the program so that the sub would navigate without a pilot, while we focused ourselves on keeping watch with our nerves on edge.

During the trip upriver, I had time to ruminate and reflect on my exchange with the Colonel, through the satellite phone that Cesar had given me; a conversation that we had before leaving, while we were still in the parking lot of El Rodadero.

"Andrei Kodina must be the key piece, Colonel; there is no doubt. If Yuri Pavenko has risked his daughter by sending her to me with the message, it is because he must be worried..." I said, still knowing that it was not true, I mean Nina, she was not his daughter; but my boss believed so and, as far as I know, Jessica had not yet corrected him. "It's important to know that Kodina is now active in the GRU, sir, that's what the message said... Who's the bugger, Colonel?"

"You are referring to Kodina, yes?"

"Naturally, sir."

There was a moment of silence at the other end of the line, during which I perceived his frustration due to my ignorance; but then I remembered where the hell I'd heard the name before.

"Don't tell me!" I cut him off before he could speak again and made me feel like an idiot. "Andrei Kodina is

Yuri's supplier on the black market, right? The architect of the Devil's Bazar in Afghanistan..."

"And the Market of Horrors in Latin America." The Colonel finished off. "Kodina is the dealer and the pair of Cossacks that I ordered you to eliminate are his men, GRU enforcers. Yuri is his salesman. Remember that Kodina and Pavenko have known each other for a long time; they were part of the Atomic Fang Division of the old KGB."

"That's *precisely* what I don't understand, sir. On the one hand, how has Andrei Kodina come to occupy a high position within the GRU? We all know the rivalry that exists between those two apparatuses of the Russian government! The most logical thing would have been for this man to end up in the higher ranks of the SVR, don't you think?"

"Absolutely."

"On the other hand, you are contradicting yourself... You are sending me to dispatch Yuri's two mercenaries, who now turn out to be Kodina's men, his partner, because *you* believe that they have been sent by him to take down Pavenko. What are we left with?"

"You still don't get it, do you, Pat?" He spoke. "We have already talked about this," he said and drew a long breath, "what you have pointed out is true. Kodina and Yuri are partners; that is not up for discussion. But theirs is a risky association, and the GRU people are not stupid, Pat, they have Yuri pegged as an important cause of the weapons leak in the Russian arsenals that I suppose they are investigating; Kodina knows that Yuri has been marked by the Department of Military Intelligence and wants to silence him before the ball bounces and hits him as well. That's all. He has already used Yuri; he has already burned him. Now he's going to take care of the loose ends..."

"Wiping the fat bastard off the map," I finished off for him.

"Exactly, that's why our informant has contacted you, although that message is not really for you."

"It's for *you*, sir."

"Correct, but it concerns you too because he knows that you will be the one to protect him from Kodina and his janissaries, as soon as I give the order. Do you know, by any chance, how the GRU deal with traitors when they catch them red-handed? No? Well, after a rough interrogation where physical torture is not ruled out and where they end up confessing *everything*, they tie them up to an iron stretcher and force them into that gigantic oven they have in the basement of The Aquarium, their headquarters at Khodinka Airport. As for your first question, the one about how Andrei Kodina was able to reach his current position within the GRU, the answer comes down to one name..."

"One name, yes sir." I repeated slowly after him.

"Vladimir Putin."

"Putin!" I heard myself mumble in disbelief. "Really, Colonel?"

"He is the *only* man in Russia who can pull off such a ruse today," my boss said. "For some time now, we have seen that he is determined to turn the defense industry into the spearhead of his government. ROSOBO-RONEXPORT, S. A. is the main state agency intermediary for the export and import of all products related to the Russian war industry. Putin is its founder; he created this new organization through a decree he signed last month to merge the company called «Rosvoorouzhenie» with «Promexport»; hence the combined name.

"Isn't it the same dog with a different collar, sir?" I asked.

"Well, yes and no... Let me explain," he said, and cleared his throat out loud; I imagined him chewing on his briar pipe, back in El Rodadero, while Bill Johnson was swinging his head and snoring in front of the television set, "the official status of ROSOBO-RONEXPORT guarantees the support of the Russian government in all its export operations. Only this corporation is licensed to supply the international market with the Russian weapons that have been authorized for export."

"Wait a minute, Colonel... Are you trying to tell me that Putin is involved in the illegal trafficking...?"

"I didn't say that, Delta," he interrupted me sharply.

"So?"

"Putin has a serious problem in getting the Russian economy moving forward, without having to resort to the iron yoke of the old Soviet system. Communist China has gone on the global market and can offer the world, with its slave labor, the most competitive market prices on any product one can imagine. In North America, for example, where the quality of consumer goods was once a preponderant factor for the average consumer, that trend has changed. Now we all look for savings, not quality. And because China produces so cheaply, we are even moving our factories to the Pacific Rim. The only thing, listen carefully, that developed countries with vast economic resources do not trust a label made in China, is..."

I saw it all very clearly without being able to specify it.

"The Defense industry," I muttered.

"Precisely. Especially the weapons of mass destruction. That is the angle that friend Putin intends to exploit for the economy of his new Russia. Aside from sticking his hands in the pie and augmenting his personal fortune, of course."

"Neither the U.S., nor the U.K., Israel, and the European Union will ever buy Russian-made weapons, sir," I told him with a firmness that I did not feel at all... because of the European Union, of course.

"Maybe not, but there is a vast market in India, for example, which are visceral enemies of China; there is also Pakistan and the entire Middle East, and perhaps the United Arab Emirates as well, many governments and dictatorships in Africa and all Latin America... Except for Colombia, of course, which has become our greatest ally nowadays, almost all the other countries repudiate us down there. Even the government of neighboring Mexico."

"True, sir." I grinned.

I was beginning to glimpse the direction things were taking, but even so, what we were dealing with was not enough to prove that Vladimir Putin, if that was the case, was behind the horrors that the irresponsible sales of black-market weapons of mass destruction could mean to America... If that could be proven, the new Russian Federation would have a lot to lose. However, the Colonel's explanation had a certain logic.

"I'm not sure that," my chief added, "Mr. Putin is personally involved in arms smuggling. The problem, I dare say, is Andrei Kodina."

"Who has been appointed chief administrator of ROSOBO-RONEXPORT by Putin," I stressed through pursed lips, "even at the risk of creating a serious disagreement with the top brass of the GRU."

"Listen, Delta," he said in a low tone, "Kodina is a bandit; he is using Yuri, or rather, he has already used him, to make money illegally at the expense of these black-market arms bazaars that affect not only us, but his own country in Eastern Europe. Putin trusts him because of his old relationship from the former KGB, but he probably doesn't know what we know…"

"Which is, sir," I interrupted him.

"The secret partnership between Mr. Kodina and the Ostrovsky Clan."

Shit, I thought.

And once again a flash of understanding suddenly illuminated my brain, and I saw *everything* clearly. A market within a market. Like the classic Russian *matryoshka*. Something very similar to what our 'heroic and righteous champion' Arnold fuckin' Feldman, the general director of the OCF, was plotting with the Ostrovsky brothers, in Aruba. While some sold the smuggled weapons, others laundered the dirty money so that no one could follow their trail.

God creates them and the devil brings them together.

"Don't be shocked if you come across friend Andrei in that shipyard, Pat," he added, surprising me even more, "I'm sure you'll find Admiral Fullerton there with his collaborators. They must be the ones directing the dismantling of the submarine."

That was something I had already thought about, but I said nothing.

"General Cedeño," he continued, "has informed me that Mr. Kodina was sighted by his spies visiting Caracas a few days ago. Although his entry into Colombia has not been recorded, he may pay us a visit at any moment; there is a long border between both countries, don't you know."

"What do you think he is in Caracas for, sir?"

"Officially, to negotiate an arms sales treaty with Hugo Chavez's regime. Every time we stop selling weapons to a dangerous dictator, the Russians appear. But I have a feeling that there may be an ulterior motive: to sound out Islamic Sword. Do you remember Ahmed?"

And upon hearing his tricky question I imagined him smiling with jovial malice. I had allowed Commander Ahmed to escape during the Cali operation, even though my boss had given me strict orders to dispatch him. But I ignored the barb and retorted: "Wait a minute, sir, would Kodina take such a big risk in his official capacity?"

"Don't be naive, Delta. He won't contact Ahmed, who is a known terrorist, that's Yuri's job. Kodina will do it with his shaman, Mr. Ali Quevach, spiritual leader of the movement and a 'respectable' Venezuelan business mogul with multiple interests in steel production, artillery factories, construction, etc., etc."

And even if it seems unbelievable, assimilating all that gave me a headache, despite how easy it was to do so listening to the reasoned way in which my boss had presented it. But I've already said that processing information and analyzing it is not my cup of tea; I don't snoop around, nor do I plan actions, I just carry them out. I wondered if Jessica — dumb question, mind you — had something to do with the investigation. *But of course!* I thought immediately, it was she who had briefed Tilson and me in Aruba about Kodina and his recent appointment by the current Prime Minister of the Russian Federation as chief administrator of ROSOBO-RONEXPORT*.

And another much more annoying question suddenly burned my insides: *Was this why my boss was separating me from Jessica? Was she more important than I to Colonel Berkowitz's new Quadrille? Was he protecting her, like one should protect the queen piece in a chess match?* If this was true, I told myself, then this project of his could be a suicide mission — that's why Karina was with me instead of her — and Jessica was not the kind of piece the old fox would allow himself the

luxury of risking in this new war.
Not even to deliver a checkmate!

*Refer to the fourth book in the series, titled *The Caribbean Sedition* (*Author's Note*).

Chapter 8

INTO THE WELL

We were almost at our destination when the halo of light that shone from the bow of our transport illuminated the grotesque grout formed by the rocks covered in river mud and sargassum. As you must know, there are more than thirty thousand known species of algae, some of which grow on the bottom of the ocean or attached to rocks, but they are also abundant in streams and lakes. They have a variety of morphologies — filamentous, laminar and calcareous algae — and they can be microscopic or reach more than fifty meters in length. The ones in front of me were closer to the largest variety; probably because they'd been planted there by men, not Nature, to serve as camouflage for the underwater installation. We left the midget sub in the same way that we had boarded it, swimming through the access hatch. After removing the bags with our gear inside, we pulled them out, swimming rhythmically towards the submerged hatch, beyond it lay a site of gargantuan dimensions, and whoever had been the architect of this waterlogged complex — probably Oscar Fullerton and his team of Seabees by the looks of it — had designed it without sparing funds. In truth, it had little to envy of a submarine base of the U.S. Navy.

Since Karina was serving as pointer, I focused on following the trail of little bubbles she was leaving behind; it was very murky down there. We crossed a flooded tunnel about thirty meters in diameter that led us to a vault, which ended where the ominous mass of treated steel was waiting, looming just a few meters ahead. As we swam up to the surface, there were lights in the ceiling of the vault, which was very high and concave, because now we had entered a kind of submerged cavity that was kept half empty by an air vacuum.

"The moment of truth has arrived, *güero*," she whispered in my ear, "shall we do this together or separately?"

"Perhaps it's better together, *chica*," I ventured hesitantly; I still had doubts about almost everything we had been ordered to do here, because that so-called "project" of my boss had become so fuckin' unreal, with so many variables, that settling it was like going step by step through a dangerous minefield. "I'll watch your six while you plant the charges and set the detonators. When you're done, just follow me and do the same while I tackle the Cossacks. But, before we apply ourselves to the task at hand, I want to do a thorough reconnaissance of the installation; okay?"

She raised her thumb in approval and winked.

"Sounds good to me. In the meantime, I'll explore the platform around the sub. Let's meet on the other side of the dais, at tower level," she muttered, and as she did so, I thought I caught a flash of a mischievous smile loaded with promise. But we were playing a very deadly game here versus some very deadly players, and when the Reaper is haunting you, one tends to say or do things one doesn't really mean.

Valentin Abramovich and his comrade-in-arms were

quartered in the security checkpoint, from where they controlled the space in which the most sensitive zones of that installation were spread. The inner concrete walls surrounding the well, from which the superstructure of the submarine and its adjacent areas protruded, was littered with scaffolding, water sleds, mini cranes and other bulky work tools. *Quite convenient for Karina*, I thought, since they could serve as cover for the girl's recon tour. The Russian mercs were attentive to the images reproduced on the screens of an ingenious electronic surveillance turret, which at its base branched into twin control panels. From my position, crouched as I was outside that oval-shaped checkpoint, I could spy on them without problems just by peering through the oblong glass panel. This was possible because the lights in the area around the checkpoint were dimmed and the vault, now that the engineers and other workers had retired to their barracks, was plunged into semi-darkness. Something very suitable for us.

Although they were quite different in their physical appearance, the Russians did have a similarity in their behavior. Watching them in action corroborated what the Colonel had been stressing from the very beginning: They were both well-trained specimens of the Russian Federation. In their files I had read that they were members of the Special Purpose troops of the Central Directorate of the Command Staff of the Armed Forces of Russia, an elite unit called *Spetsnaz GRU*, which answers exclusively to the Department of Military Intelligence of the Russian Army. This detachment, the file said, was founded in 1949 as a group of fighters well prepared for the Cold War, because, unlike the average Soviet soldier, their tasks always turned out to be clandestine ops in which wet affairs and acts of sabotage on a greater or lesser scale, were carried out behind enemy lines. In other words, they were not shock troops; they did not fight head-on and in open battlefields, but from afar and in the shadows.

People like us.

Abramovich was of medium height, with coarse black hair and the swarthy skin one often finds in natives of the Eurasian republics. Black, slanted eyes, separated by a pronounced nasal appendage, which ended in dilated nostrils. His lips were thick, with deep corners. His body was hairless or seemed to be. He had high cheekbones and a slightly sunken chin. A lush tuft of black hair festooned his forehead, which was narrow and unwrinkled. He was probably not a great thinker, perhaps for that reason I marked him as Heckle. His buddy would be Jeckle.

His partner-in-crime (this one was sitting by the left dashboard of the turret, sipping from a compact flask of vodka) was Misha Sokolov, the White Russian. A mountain of muscles with straight blond hair. He had a broad face with a bulbous nose, a square chin, a bushy moustache that ran down his cheeks like the handlebars of a bicycle; a bull's neck; bright blue eyes and a massive forehead: a Slavic narwhal. The file gave him a height of 6'4 and a weight of 280 pounds: a true man-mountain trained to kill. He reminded me of Goliath. *

Of course, this wasn't the first time I'd had to deal with one of these titans — I'd come across several Slavic mammoths during my clashes with Russian Mafia killers — but the advantage I thought I had over these two talking magpies (as with Goliath) was precisely that they were all military-schooled: meaning, they were predictable. All pros adhere to a standard code of conduct. There are minor variations based on the region of the globe where they are forged, but the profession itself is universal. Knowing how Russian Special Forces operate gave me a clue, however small. In fact, I was more worried about the others, those the Colonel hadn't mentioned to Karina: Andrei Kodina, for one; Yuri Pavenko and his beautiful gunwoman; Admiral Fullerton and his entourage of engineers; and that bloody Commander Ahmed, if he dared to show himself.

During the time we spent reviewing the few details that were given to us about the Enigma-3 Project, Karina always believed that she had everything under control, when the truth is that Miss Reyes was unaware of the most important points. Enigma-3 was an operation supported by Colombian Army personnel, not so much out of loyalty to good old Uncle Sam, but because of the proximity of the terrorist camp that Islamic Sword had set up right under their noses, on the outskirts of the borders with the now hostile government of neighboring Venezuela. That worried them a *lot*. They were also concerned about the presence of the enormous American attack sub that was skulking in the deep murky waters of the Magdalena River, and what this nuclear-powered mechanical monster (if fallen into the wrong hands) could mean for the control of the most important river artery in their entire country....

For the Colombian government, it has become imperative to maintain a tight reign over the waters of the Magdalena River since guerrilla violence had broken out in the country; although some claim that this has always been the case, since the times of the *Conquistadores*. The Magdalena River is a strategic area that remains in the sight of all insurgent groups. The National Liberation Army (ELN), for instance, has already tried to own it without much success. But the day that one of the best-armed guerrilla armies in the country manages to seize a weapon of such magnitude, the military bases that protect this key nautical corridor

— not to mention all Colombia and other nations in the hemisphere — will be in grave danger and control of national commerce will fall into the terrorists' hands.

When river transport began its development subsidized by the state in Colombia, the regional trade dependence on the Magdalena River grew dramatically. Traveling on its waters became unavoidable, because they flow north between the eastern and central mountain ranges of the Colombian Andes, crossing the northern region of the so-called Lowlands. But it does not stop there, of course, its waters continue to advance until they merge with those of the Cauca River, before flowing into the Caribbean Sea. Therefore, cities such as Neiva, Girardot, Honda, La Dorada, Puerto Boyacá, Puerto Berrio, Santa Cruz de Mompox and Barrancabermeja, Magangué and Barranquilla, absolutely *all* of them depend on it. It reaches Cundinamarca and Tolima and serves as a drainage basin for other important bodies of water such as the Páez River, the Saldaña, the La Miel River, the Nare and the San Jorge. But these are only the ones that lie west of the Magdalena. To the east it is linked to six or seven other waterways. Even in the 16th century, the Spanish conquistadors used it to cross impenetrable mountain forests on their way to the interior, as it was the only transport route that connected Bogotá with the Caribbean port of Cartagena de Indias, and then Europe.

Get the picture now?

To all I've said, I must add that the most productive fishing areas in all of Colombia converge in its basin, because its entirety covers twenty-four percent of the national territory, where sixty-six percent of the population resides; that is why no government, in its right mind, allows such a possession to be taken away from their hands.

As I mulled all this over, crouching in my hiding place, my conscience was aching, believe me, and that cynical grimace, typical of my boss, did not cease to torment me as I crossed the valley of shadows into which my soul was sinking. That was what the proud Miss Reyes did not know; she never imagined that she was being used by my Col. Berkowitz as cannon fodder, in case the caper went astray. *You can sacrifice her, Delta,* I seemed to hear him saying, without giving much thought to the matter. *Use her as bait to hunt down the Russians...* That was why he had left Jessica out. His rigid, chauvinistic mind had never considered that I might be the one to fall for it... But life gives us all surprises, you know. And thinking about what my next step would be, I suddenly noticed with apprehension something I should have noted from the very beginning.

No one was dismantling the Ohio-class sub.

I left the spot next to the checkpoint and began to move, very cautiously, towards the place where I'd agreed to meet Karina. I was forced to go around the platform surrounding the well — something that you can say faster than it's done — because I had to tread carefully so as not to set off the alarms of possible motion sensors. When I finally reached her side, the apprehensive look with which she greeted me confirmed that she had already noticed the same thing I had.

"I can't blow it up, Delta," she whispered in my ear and showed me the little screen on her tablet, "there are nukes on this bloody monster!"

I crouched down in front of her, who was squatted behind a loading tractor in the shadow of the steel-skinned leviathan, its back and tower jutting out of the pit, and I pressed myself against Karina as much as I could, covering her smaller hands with mine, around the small screen of the tablet to block its glare. What she was now showing me was a comprehensive blueprint of an Ohio-class attack submarine of the U.S. Navy.

The detailed diagram of the ship's interior was sectioned and numbered in such a way that was very clear to the observer. Section (1), for example, corresponded to the dome where the bow sonar was installed: a device that sends pulses of sound waves through the water. When these pulses hit objects such as other ships, or fish within its radius, even vegetation or the bottom, they are reflected to the surface. This device serves to measure the time it takes for the sound wave to descend, hit an object and then bounce back. Section (2) was a compartment that housed the rapid immersion tanks. Section (3) was the computer room. Section (4) corresponded to the communications room, followed by Section (5) the sonar chamber where the experts who listen to and analyze the sounds captured by the waves work. Section (6) was the ship's command center, just below the periscope and the submarine's tower, and Section (7) the navigation center. That's why Karina had planned to put C-4 explosive charges in the tower, to disable the brain of the mechanical leviathan. And so, one section after another followed, until reaching the last one numbered Section (17) in the diagram, the one that really changed things for us: the missile compartment.

There were twenty-four ICBMs in total, damn it... twenty-four Intercontinental Ballistic Missiles, of the *Trident II D5* SLBM type, capable of carrying up to twelve nuclear bombs per warhead (twelve each, for God's sake!) of the W88 type, each with 475 kilotons and a range of 6,100 nautical miles, which is equivalent to 11,300 kilometers. The realization of this terrified me all at once.

I suddenly felt nauseous, and a feverish sensation crept up my spine until it burned into my brain. *What the hell was this!* Was the Colonel aware that Fullerton's sub was pregnant? Did Admiral Seltzer and the other Joint Chiefs know? With just one of these birds flying, they could easily reach the very center of Washington... but also Moscow. *Did the GRU know this? Was that why they'd sent two of their operatives? Was this the reason why General Cedeño had an elite commando unit standing nearby, waiting for a signal to assault this bloody shipyard and ensure the confiscation of such a formidable doomsday weapon?* The price of this infernal toy, even without its deadly payload, was two billion dollars. *Two billion*, for Christ's sake! And each bloody missile cost about thirty million... *Who the hell had that much money to pay for all this?!*

Karina and I looked at each other in silence, shivering from the mugginess and the cold that the Grim Reaper drags along when it begins to stalk you. And together we wished that the earth would open at our feet and swallow us both alive...

But then I got an idea.

Misha Sokolov (alias Jeckel) was so used to dealing with the routine of panning the different sectors of the facility — you really had to be crazy to infiltrate the place — that he almost couldn't believe the image that suddenly materialized on the screens of the video cameras that focused on the back of the submarine: a furtive silhouette, dressed in black with the typical clothing of the combat swimmer.

"*Fuck!*" Jeckel cursed out loud in Russian. "Hey, Val, we've got company! Get your ass over here..."

Abramovich (alias Heckel) jumped off the rotating stool with the swiftness of a wild cat and when he stopped next to his partner, his right hand was already holding the handle of an amphibious assault rifle «ASM-DT».

"What's going on, partner, why all the fuss?"

"Why all the fuss?! Check this out!" Jeckel punched a few keys on the dashboard pad to enlarge one of the images of the well, and both men watched as an amorphous shadow glided over the big ship's back, advancing towards the submarine's tower.

"Hey! What the hell is this!" Heckel burst out. "Aren't the American engineers taking a break?"

"They are. This one looks like an intruder... Give me a moment to sharpen up the image. Shit, it's a woman!"

Heckel looked closely and, indeed, he noticed the rounded protuberances that expanded the neoprene jacket in the bust area, now shiny from the humidity.

"There you have an enhancement," Jeckel spat.

Heckel studied the magnified image for a few more seconds and then pursed his lips in an energic rictus. "Holy Moscow!!" he hissed, raising his eyebrows, "those are tits, *tovarisch*!"

"*Da*. And some tits they are!" Jeckel fiercely agreed. "This bloody gal is checking out the sub, Val, look!!"

"Call the boss and brief him on the situation. I'll go get her."

But at this point that didn't matter, because the two talking magpies were about to embark on the "great journey" from which no one ever returned.

<hr>

*Refer to the second volume in the series, titled *Red Goliath* (*Author's Note*).

THE KREMLIN'S RUSE

Part Three

*C*hapter **9**

JACK BULL, NRO

The moment called for precise, unwavering action, though I confess that I would have liked to know who the real boss was (Kodina? Pavenko? Admiral Fullerton?) but the pair of Russian killers waiting for me were the kind you must give your full attention to and get a head start on them to defeat them. The only element I had left to thrash them (before they raised the alarm throughout the facility, or worse, came for me) was the element of surprise. Since neither of them expected to find me there, I stooped and quickly entered the checkpoint, arms outstretched out front holding my silenced pistol in both hands, firing at them.

Heckel fell first, having been on his way to the door at the exact moment I went in. I got two shots off into that narrow, wrinkle-free forehead of his before he could aim his rifle in my direction, and when the man collapsed bleeding from his wounds, he was still holding the ASM-DT in his hands. Luckily, the weapon did not go off. The last thing I needed, in those critical moments, was a furious burst of 5.45-millimeter slugs ricocheting off the metal roof and walls of the checkpoint.

I took the opportunity to shift my attention from the

dead Russie to Sokolov, who had now turned in his chair to face me as he sensed his partner's collapse. I also aimed at his head because the distance separating us inside the checkpoint was favorable — between fifteen and twenty yards — and the SW22 *Victory* I carried, being of light caliber and having a long and heavy barrel, is one of the most accurate target pistols in the world. To top off my good fortune, his head was almost as bulky as a thoroughbred's, more than an easy target at that distance for an expert marksman. I indulged myself with him. First, I put a bullet in each eye socket, followed by two in the throat and then I kept pulling the trigger until the remaining four .22LR slugs were grouped in the heart area. The gun's slide locked back with a metallic click as the last of the ten shots in the magazine was fired. Sokolov took his hands to his chest and collapsed, tipping over the swivel on which he was sitting. I quickly exchanged the empty magazine for a fresh one and unlocked the slide, feeding the first round into the chamber.

Then I saw the telephone handset dangling from the thick cord that connected it to its base; it was swaying slightly. A voice mixed with static was ranting in a foreign language that sounded like Russian to me. I took a couple of steps back, raised my gun and put four bullets in my first victim's torso, just to make sure he would never give me trouble again, and then approached the swinging handset. I took it in my left hand and held it carefully to my ear. The voice speaking on the other end of the connection suddenly went silent, giving me no time to identify it. I gently returned the handset to its base and drew a long breath. A noise behind me alerted me that someone had just entered the checkpoint. I expected it to be Karina, but when I turned on my heels to face my partner, I was confronted by a short young man in a white lab coat, carrying a flat electronic board under his left armpit and a peculiar metal briefcase in his left.

The most significant thing was that, in his right hand, he was holding a handgun with a silencer. And he was aiming the firearm straight at me.

"Uh, uh... stay cool," he cut me off with a whisper that sounded more threatening than the roar of an angry lion. "Be sure not to make a sudden move. Leave the gun arm dangling, gramps. I want the barrel of your pistol pointed at the floor now; that's it. Now bring your other hand up with your palm facing the ceiling. Careful, eh."

I obeyed, of course. The firmness with which the kid held his gun, the deadliness reflected in his apathetic gaze and the serenity he showed before the corpses that surrounded us, each swimming in a pool of blood that was now beginning to spread all over the floor, was more than enough to convince me that this character — no matter how young he looked — was a seasoned pro.

The question that gnawed at my insides was: Why the hell was he dressed like a technician?

"Is there anyone else with you, grandpa, or are you here alone?" he asked.

I tried to appear composed as I denied the presence of a companion, but the boy caught a movement on one of the screens of the surveillance console that the late Misha Sokolov had been monitoring and squinted his eyelids. His brow furrowed as we both watched Karina climb down from the submarine's tower.

"Wow, nice couple. You have good taste, old man," he whispered, but his voice was as dry and cold as an iceberg. There was not the slightest hint of humor in it. Not even the satirical kind.

"You're too young to be so serious, kid, don't you think?" I grinned. "Hey, are you related to Chuck

Norris?" I added, and immediately realized that this was a question he'd been asked before. Probably countless times. He bore a striking resemblance to the actor.

"Yeah, I'm his father," he replied dryly, but this young man wasn't even close to thirty. I estimated him at twenty-four, or maybe twenty-five, he was a contemporary of Jessica.

"More like his son, you mean," I smiled reluctantly, "or maybe a grandson. You really look like him, you know. What, are you a martial artist also?"

"You can say that, grandpa. Among other things."

Well, I'd figured as much. This new generation of secret agents are all nearly perfect. I looked at him again and noticed that his physiognomy — especially his face — was beginning to spark flashes of images in my lazy memory, and I suddenly realized that his face was indeed familiar to me. It was a face I'd come across in the CI5 Shared Archives, not in action films.

"You are Jackson Bull, of course," I hissed, closing my eyelids for a split second and shaking my head from side to side. "Hell, if we continue to operate blindfolded, the day is not far off when we start shooting each other in the field, by mistake."

This time my words caused a reaction. His cold grey eyes narrowed further, giving his countenance a sudden hardness.

Lone Wolf McQuade, I thought, and at that moment Karina Reyes sneaked up into the checkpoint holding her silenced pistol in both hands.

"Put the gun down, *pimpollo*!" she spat, and my balls shrank. The last thing we needed at this point was to get into a gunfight with an operator of the NRO's Nuclear Counterproliferation Center, one of our two closest allies in the entire array of the U.S. government's security forces: the other being the FBI. Even if he had orders to hunt down Yuri Pavenko and I had orders to do everything I could to stop that from happening, up to the point of *eliminating* him, if necessary.

Jackson Bull belonged to the NRO.

"It's all right, *querida*," I told her. "The kiddo is a U.S. government agent."

"A G-man, you say? Maybe he is, but he's pointing his gun at *you,*" Karina argued, and she was right.

"But that is because he doesn't know who we are yet, of course."

"And who are *you*, may I ask?" Jack growled, but his body language told me he wasn't going to shoot us; at least not before we got things straightened out.

"I work with the OCF, whiz kid," I replied, "please note I said with and not for."

"The OCF has no say in this caper, grandpa; this is a matter that only concerns the U.S. Navy and the ONR, because Yuri Pavenko is involved..." he forgot about me for a moment and pointed the barrel of his gun in the direction of where the submarine was anchored, "and that steel monster you see there too. *Especially* the twenty-four ICBMs it carries in its belly with their multiple warheads. The torpedoes interest me too, of course, but I can live without those," he replied with calculated aplomb, though his gun came back to aim in my direction.

"Pavenko is on our agenda too," I pointed out.

"Who are *you*, what's your name?" He asked.

"My real name won't tell you anything, but you can ask around for Agent Delta. It's my code name."

"Agent Delta..." he repeated, "and *whom* may I ask for references on you, grandpa?"

The whole thing was getting a bit tiresome, not to mention ridiculous, perhaps it would be better to shoot it out with him — there were two of us now against just him — but I resigned myself to having a little patience with the newer generations. Tough work, though.

"You know Samuel Norwood? He's part of a unit that fights organized crime in the Bureau. Sam is currently stationed in the Caribbean, but when I first met him, he was working with a covert Bureau counterintelligence group in Washington, D.C. At present, Sam's base is an electronic tracking station that operates secretly out of one of the private hangars at Opa Locka Executive Airport in Miami, claiming to be a charter flight agency to the Caribbean islands. They lease light aircraft and four-seater helicopters with or without a pilot."

He said nothing.

"If Norwood is not available," I went on, "ask for Len Greenwald or Bruce Benson then. They both work with him."

"I know Sam; what's the name of this charter flying company?" He asked to test me, because I bet my balls the kid already knew that.

"The Royal Sky Flying Group, Ltd., if I remember correctly. It's listed in the legal records as a British firm doing business at Miami International Airport," I added. "Talk to Sam if you like, son, but carry on, will you? We've got some *serious* matters to attend to here."

I signaled Miss Reyes to put her gun down. She took her time in doing so, but in the end, she gave me the benefit of doubt. In any case, the girl lowered her silenced Victory pistol but did not put it away; I sensed that she was very uptight. Can't say I blame her; I felt the same.

The funny thing was that this Jack Bullshit character didn't look nervous at all. I marveled at the intense composure and self-confidence of this young man with rosy, leathery skin and a head of straight blond hair that matched his bushy blond beard and moustache. I bet he had played college football at some Midwestern university and had probably graduated with honors from MIT — just like Jessica.

Screw them all, for fuck's sake! I reflected with some bitterness. I was getting fed up with this bloody new Millenium age where advanced technology and politically correctness ruled.

Yeah... *Bloody fuckers!*

Chapter 10

BETTER RUN THAN DIE

Almost an hour before Karina was detected at the well by the now dead Russian mercs, in one of the most luxurious suites overlooking the sea in that splendid beach resort called El Rodadero, Nina Tetriak danced lasciviously for Yuri, swaying her beautiful young body while she stripped off a short, tight black dress to the sound of the exotic Gypsy tunes she enjoyed so much. The melodies that, as a child, she'd listened to with her parents when they all were part of a circus show in old Soviet Moscow. The dress was the same sexy piece she'd been wearing when she'd intercepted me at the hotel's parking lot to deliver the message about Andrei Kodina.

With his fat rolls encased in a white plush dressing gown, flaunting the hotel monogram embroidered in gold over the heart, Yuri Pavenko almost drooled as he stared at the reflection of Nina's enchanting figure in the large oval moon of the dressing table mirror. Eyes ecstatic with overflowing lust, his pulse racing from all the cocaine he'd sniffed just seconds before, the Russian arms dealer admired his young nymph while taking small sips of vodka. When the girl finally freed her breasts and showed him her fully erect nipples, protruding from the two perfect cones of gelatinous flesh she had for mammary glands, old Yuri could stand it no longer and shivered as he approached her. The Gypsy she-devil was driving him nuts! So did pure coke and vodka. He'd been sucking on one of the most expensive bottles available abroad at that time, the Ultra Vodka brand, also labeled The Jewel of Russia. It had cost a little more than a hundred dollars, much more than the twenty-one-dollar bottle of Belvedere, or the twenty-six dollars he paid for Stolichnaya, which he thought was already a lot.

But Comrade Yuri had always been a hedonist and a sybarite since I first met him, almost two decades ago*; living ten years in a great cosmopolitan city famous the world over for luxury, vice, and excess, like Manhattan, had marked him for life. New York, like Paris, Madrid and Rome, often has that effect on people.

"Oh, Nina..." he gasped.

His husky voice, laden with the doughy breath that gave off a whiff of alcohol, came in waves to the beautiful young woman, when she suddenly felt the soft touch of the man's puffy hands as they cupped each one of her quivering breasts. Yuri fiddled with that glorious pair of knockers and Nina smiled in pure delight, for it pleased her to know she was coveted by him and contemplated the spell her charms cast on this old steppe bear, as wicked as he was adorable when surrendered to her feet. Pavenko's hands worked her expertly, drawing sparks to the tips of her nipples as he gently squeezed them between thick fingers, and she licked her lips with pleasure in his lap, bucking her bottom to dig into his groin and rub her creamy bums against his erection... Yuri could take no more and clutching a lock of her hair in one fist, he forced Nina's head back and kissed her long, sensual neck. He tore off her half-removed dress, lifted her in his arms and carried her to bed. He threw her face up on the foam mattress and stripping off his dressing gown, Yuri parted her legs and plunged himself in between them.

Nina howled like a she-wolf to the moon, but he planted a kiss on her mouth that sealed her lips and soon began grunting and pumping his full corpulence into her. She moaned and raised her hips to meet his thrusts with her legs spread as wide as she could and hugging her man's powerful neck, until the fat bastard turned her upside down and urged her to get on all fours before mounting her. They were in the middle of a hectic wild ride when the loud ringing of the satellite phone startled them.

Yuri shot a murderous glance at the darned device, which lay on its base next to the bed, he considered smashing it to smithereens by banging it against the flagstone floor. Then his countenance registered apprehension and without leaving his diva's body he reached out with a hairy hand and answered the call.

"What do you want?" he growled into the mouthpiece.

His countenance showed apprehension when Misha Sokolov informed him that a female intruder had breached the shipyard's security and was now snooping around the compound.

"God damn it!" roared Pavenko, which, by the way, was just pure show, since he'd been forewarned that something like this was bound to happen. "What the hell are you calling me for, you useless fuck? Get off your ass and hunt the bitch down."

"We're on it, boss, but you gave orders to contact you immediately in case of a breach. Val is already going after her..."

"You dumb son of a bitch!? She may not be alone! Take her alive, goddamn it! She and everyone with her! I want to know who the hell sent them!" Yuri shouted into the phone before abruptly cutting off the call.

Then he felt his swollen manhood, still buried deep inside Nina, begin to deflate and he abruptly pulled away from the girl, cursing under his breath. The GRU buggers had fucked up his day. Now he had a lot to worry about and the best thing he could do was to flee Barranquilla as soon as possible. He wasn't kidding himself, the next call that son of a bitch Sokolov would make would be to his real boss to fill him in and that bastard Kodina would immediately suspect Yuri, the only one involved who had already collected his commission for the deal in advance: the one who had the least to lose!

Pavenko probably never realized it, but it was my timely intervention in eliminating the GRU assassins which saved his life. Had Kodina found out about the assault to the well while passing through Caracas, Nina and Yuri would never have escaped Colombia alive; that much is certain. After all, the arms dealer must've figured as he jumped out of bed to hurriedly get dressed, better run than die!

*Refer to the first volume in the series, entitled *The Quadrille* (*Author's Note*).

Chapter 11

THE ULTIMATE WEAPON

It wasn't necessary for Jack Bull to call Agent Norwood to verify my identity over the phone; Sam did it in person, because it turned out that the FBI's albino champion was also on the premises, though I didn't know it. I learned of his presence in the grotto when the overly suspicious NRO kid escorted us at gunpoint to the barracks, where Admiral Fullerton's entire engineering team and the rest of the hired help had been lodged. To my pleasant surprise, Sam was accompanied by Agents Greenwald and Benson, the pair of "cleaners" who had roasted alive the Russian mobsters who'd ambushed us at Divi Beach during Operation Parasol, in Aruba. *

Well, it made sense, didn't it? If I hadn't been able to neutralize the two GRU magpies, Greenwald and Benson would've taken care of them. In military jargon, that's called Plan B. It was at that point in time that I began to realize that my boss's little project had ceased to be just that — his project — and that the entire affair had evolved into a real Black Bag operation fully sanctioned by some U.S. government security agencies and no longer a personal venture of his, as I'd been told at the beginning. In any case, project or not, I was facing the mother of all missions; this was not the simple elimination of two enemy agents and a small band of

125

ingrates militating on our own side — and it was easy to understand why, dammit: we had to *secure* the twenty-four ICBMs loaded with multiple warheads and put everything back in safe storage.

"Hey, guys," I greeted them, a genuine feeling of satisfaction settling in my soul. It was a joy to be among friends again, or at least allies. And for the first time since Enigma 3 had begun to roll, I sensed that things were starting to get on track.

Sam came to meet me as soon as he saw us arrive and shook my hand effusively; Greenwald and Benson followed suit, although less effusively, which didn't worry me in the least because I know that "cleaners" are not naturally affable guys and when they're mobilized it's not precisely to do diplomacy, but to kick ass and bust the balls of whoever they are ordered to. But even so, both toughies attested to Jack that I was who I said I was and not an impostor. When it was my turn, I introduced Karina to them as my partner-in-crime for this caper and that was it.

The big surprise came later.

Miss Reyes listened to me patiently — though, in truth, she seemed a bit disappointed — when, after a brief consultation with Agent Norwood, I was forced to tell her that the time had come to part ways. Her original mission, I explained, had been aborted and her participation was not required for the next maneuver, only mine. The beautiful brunette listened resignedly and replied that she didn't feel very comfortable with the turn of events, since the Colonel had paid her a hefty advance for blowing up of the sub and, at this stage of the game, she was not contemplating returning the money. I cut her off by saying that it was not necessary, but I did advise her to contact my boss as soon as she could and to remain available for a reasonable period of time for any contingency that might arise, since it was likely that the Colonel would need her services again shortly and that would be her opportunity to earn the collected pay. I wasn't wrong in assuming that; but that's another story.

"*Vaya con Dios*, my *güero...*" she said, winking at me, and that was the last thing I heard from her mouth before she took off.

"You as well, my *morenaza,*" I replied, returning the wink, and we both smiled at the end of the exchange.

I helped her load all the luggage we had brought in on Coco's sub, except for my weapons, the ammo that belonged to me and the satellite phone Cesar had given me in El Rodadero. After that I watched her sail away in the midget submarine, overcome by a certain feeling of nostalgia that I could not explain; I suppose that her premature departure made me realize, despite our differences, how much I liked the girl. Minutes later, I met with Sam and Jack to discuss what our next move would be, while Greenwald and Benson busied themselves resuscitating Admiral Fullerton and his crew, who had been drugged during dinnertime.

"Now, for your peace of mind," Sam spoke, addressing me, "I can assure you that we are all working together on this."

"By all," Jack clarified, "we mean the NRO, the FBI and U.S. Navy Intelligence. And, of course, your little anonymous unit. But I repeat: the OCF is not a part of this."

"What friend Jack means is that only Col. Berkowitz's outfit has been added to the stew, so, you can relax. We have already contacted him to brief him on your situation, okay?"

"I hear you, Sam," I grinned and let my shoulders slump to show him that his words had lifted a big weight off my shoulders, "the truth is that I was worried about having to explain to the Colonel that the only order of his that I was able to satisfy was... well, you know. There were other names on the list he'd given me, but I haven't come across any of their owners, yet."

"If you mean the Islamic Sword guerrillas, don't sweat it, Delta, they're not involved in this."

"Oh, they're not? Really!" I exclaimed, showing astonishment at his revelation. "Are you *sure* about that, Sam? The Colombians suspect those sons of bitches are..."

He shook his head emphatically. "Not in this case. You see, putting the Ohio-class for sale on the black market was only a ruse, Delta; it's been a very well-planned deception. Admiral Fullerton was paid for something else." Norwood said, looking me straight in the eye.

"What *fucking* else, Sam?" I asked, now showing skepticism, because what Norwood was saying was very different from what the Colonel had fed me.

"The notion of sacrificing his boat and part of the crew," answered Jack Bull for him, who undoubtedly was also aware of the charade. At times it even seemed to be Jack, and not Sam, the one calling the shots in this operation. The only moron who had ever made it here with a blindfold on was me, but that's not unusual when you work for Marlon Berkowitz. The Colonel always made us play the piece by ear.

"Sacrifice his boat..." I repeated doubtfully. "Sacrifice the Ohio-class to *whom*, for God's sake?!"

"To the Russian navy, of course; to an Akula-class submarine that is currently waiting for it somewhere in the depths of the Atlantic, presumably to put it out of commission. The Russians will make it *disappear* so they can escort it all the way to Russia without anyone ever suspecting foul play and have a team of GRU naval engineers dismantle it there and analyze it piece by piece. How do you think these bastards have progressed so much in undersea warfare in the last few years?"

"Don't fuck with me, Jack, *no one* will believe that!" I snapped.

"Precisely!" Sam hastened to interject. "*That*'s the idea. What do you think people will believe?"

"I don't know, Sam... Anything but *that!*"

"They will believe," said Sam rather stoically, "that a Russian Akula has slayed our Ohio-class, and the notion will incite many countries to decide on Russian weapons instead of investing in American weapons. Of course, the Russian government will never admit in public that its navy had anything to do with the disappearance of the American sub, you know how these things are," he grinned mischievously. "Neither will we admit having anything to do with the *disappearance* of that Akula either... Will we, Jack?"

"Absolutely not," responded NRO's Agent Bull very seriously. I've already mentioned that he was a humorless prick.

"I'm beginning to perceive the strategy behind all this," I added immediately. "Indeed, the Colonel suspected something like this from the beginning."

And as I said this, I recalled my chief's words when he first approached me to talk about the project: *I'm inclined to believe that they want to convince us of their invincibility*, he'd said, referring to the Russian Akulas, *to scare us and force us to waste resources on unbridled defensive measures.* How far away that day seemed to me now, when we had talked in his office at the CI5 headquarters building in Midtown Miami. But, despite everything that had been said, there were still doubts in my mind; especially about Pavenko's role in the big scheme…

"But how can you be so sure that it's a ruse? What about Yuri Pavenko?" I asked Sam.

"He was also fooled, Delta, that much is obvious, isn't it? He was played by Andrei Kodina, who made Yuri believe that the Ohio-class was being hijacked to be dismantled and *sold* in the black market, and even paid him a commission in advance for brokering the deal, so Pavenko wouldn't suspect a thing. Do you understand? It was an extremely well-planned move from the beginning.

"First, Putin puts Kodina in a high position within the Department of Military Intelligence of the Russian Federation, which justifies his interest in weapons of mass destruction and gives him unlimited influence in some arsenals. Kodina strengthens his ties with Yuri, making him believe that they can do business under the table and establishes trust with him by making certain concessions, surely authorized by the big man in the Kremlin, to create an 'unconscious agent,' one who has no idea that he has become one.…"

The same thing that the Colonel had done with old Yuri, only using different methods and for very different purposes, I reflected.

"So, if what you're saying is true, this has all been orchestrated by Putin and his advisers, right?" I spoke.

"It seems so; it's a brilliant move, don't you agree? Pure Russian chess."

"It is, without a doubt, but it's an extremely risky one, Sam. Does this guy really dare to do so?"

"The risks have been calculated, Delta. Mr. Putin knows that we will not go to a nuclear confrontation for the mere disappearance of a submarine; in fact, no one ever has," Jack intervened, signaling Sam to allow him to speak.

"Analyze what I'm about to tell you, Delta: statistics show that every so often an attack submarine disappears or breaks down at the bottom of the ocean. To date, there have been four recorded incidents during the Cold War period, which occurred when tensions between East and West were much more tense than they're at present and neither side dared to launch the first strike.

"On April 10, 1963, the first nuclear submarine, the *USS Thresher*, designated by the Navy as SSN-593, disappeared while its crew, we are talking about one hundred and twenty-nine men including the ship's commander, conducted deep-diving maneuvers about three hundred and fifty kilometers east of Boston, Massachusetts..." he paused while seeming to remember something. "Sorry, the *Thresher* was not the first one," he corrected himself immediately, "although it was the *first* of the American submarines to vanish, before that there was a French sub, the *Surcouf*, which was lost in Caribbean waters in 1942 with a crew of one hundred and thirty sailors."

He stopped and grinned at me. I drew a long breath and said nothing.

"In 1968, on May 22nd to be exact, the second American submarine disappeared, which is the third on the list: the *USS Scorpion*, a ship classified by our Navy as SSN-589; it had ninety-nine men on board, including its commander. The causes of this incident, like its predecessor, the *USS Thresher*, remain a mystery. The fourth ship to disappear is a Russian submarine of the Oscar-class, the *Kursk*, designated by the Russian Navy as K-141. The *Kursk* was considered invincible by its builders, the pride of the Russian Navy with its sixteen thousand tons. It measured twice the size of a Jumbo 747 aircraft and was considered the most powerful nuclear sub in the entire Russian Northern Fleet.

However," here he paused to smile with jovial malice, "the ship sank only a few months ago and did so in a matter of minutes in the Barents Sea — also during military maneuvers. At the time of this tragedy, there were 118 sailors on board, including their commander. By the way, Mr. Putin was forced to appear in public before the press and face the questions that many relatives of the missing crew members had."

"Putin," I said frowning, "*again*... It's beginning to sound like the little red man's retribution."

"The point I want to stress, Agent Delta, is that *no one* is going to start a nuclear war just because one more sub is missing; be it Russian, Chinese, or American. If there is no nation claiming responsibility for causing the incident. After all, accidents do happen, don't they, and at sea, just as in the skies, they're almost always fatal."

"Very well stated," I conceded, before sighing, "but let me remind you that before Fullerton's sub, there were two others that went missing."

"Two that were recovered quickly and discreetly; no one has found out about them except us and those involved. I'm told that none of them survived, so...."

Norwood grinned at me. "It never made the news, Pat."

"Touché." I grinned.

"Also," Jack Bull went on, the kid seemed to be a walking encyclopedia on naval matters, "look carefully at the sub they have targeted for their prank: none other than an Ohio-class, the largest and most dangerous in the entire U.S. Navy: our ultimate weapon. After the invincible *Kursk* was ridiculed before the eyes of the entire world, it's obvious that, to make a dramatic impact with which to recover, our Ohio-class is the ideal choice. But there is something curious that most people don't know. All eighteen Ohio-class submarines in our

Navy are already in the process of being replaced. The new generation is the Columbia-class, so we can afford to lose one Ohio without having to go to war over it. Are you getting the picture? It's all been calculated."

"Yeah," I nodded.

"Check out the timetable. They lose the *Kursk* in August of the current year and just a few days ago, in November, President Putin signs a decree to create ROSOBO-RONEXPORT and announce it to the world as the *only* agency authorized in Russia to sell heavy armament and all kinds of lesser weapons... Do you know why it's the only one? Because it is controlled by the State, or rather, by the military."

"Which is the same as to say Mr. Putin himself."

"Precisely."

"And then he turns around and places Andrei Kodina, a man who is loyal to him and whom he knows well from his years as a former KGB agent, in the highest position of that agency. Kodina has been deceiving Pavenko and if we ever got suspicious," I added with a twisted smile, "we would conclude that his strategy is to throw Yuri to the wolves of their military intelligence, making them believe that this fat, hoarse, well-off son of a bitch is the one behind the contraband detected in their arsenals. Which is true, of course, there's no denying that Yuri has gotten this far with the underhanded assistance of the big boss himself: Andrei Kodina."

"Eureka," Jackson Bull hissed, "now you got it."

"As Agent Bull says," Norwood stepped in, "every move has been coldly calculated by the Kremlin gang, as they have a lot to gain if the gambit works out for them."

Well, put in that way everything fit together, of course, and there was a moment when the Colonel's voice resonated again in my memory tunnel: *Kodina knows that Yuri has been marked by the Department of*

Military Intelligence and intends to silence him before the ball bounces and spreads... He has already used him, he has already burned him, now he must tighten all the loose ends.

It couldn't have been summed up better.

And Pavenko had noticed his precarious situation, that's why he'd sent Nina over to meet me in El Rodadero with his little message for the Colonel....

Yeah, as I said before, it all made sense now.

Witnessing how Enigma 3 ended, the importance of the NRO lad in this new kind of war which the New World Order has brought us, became abundantly clear to me. His intervention — though I confess it made me feel uncomfortable, because I must admit that his talents and preparation were far superior to mine — was crucial in the complicated maneuver.

The peculiar briefcase he carried connected to an electronic board was plugged into a port of the Ohio-class sub's central computer. Using some kind of application (I think that's what he called it, but it's a computer program to you) Jackson Bull was able to navigate the U.S. Navy's iron leviathan almost by himself. I say *almost* because to complement those functions that said application did not perform, the lives of Admiral Fullerton and the men in his crew were preserved, momentarily; Greenwald, Benson and I took charge of watching them very closely during the process. But the program Jack was using was stacked with defense maneuvers' codes, attack commands and evasion tactics. No one cared to explain to me how this new technology worked, or who had invented it, for that matter. I just assumed it was another one of those advanced-weapons systems that the Pentagon is always developing to improve our arsenal. But there is no doubt that the magic worked, even if it seemed more like something out of a sci-fi novel or a Tom Clancy techno-thriller than fact.

Sam took it upon himself to convince Admiral Fullerton that it would be more profitable to cooperate, offering him a secret pact that would guarantee presidential immunity to him and his brethren, if they all willingly collaborated in the disappearance of the Russian Akula awaiting us at the bottom of the sea. As expected, the Admiral accepted; at this point, what other choice did he have? We marched them aboard the ship, and I took charge of Oscar Fullerton myself; Greenwald and Benson divided up the rest of the crew. We had the burdensome job of shepherding a flock of betrayers we could not execute until they served our purpose, but that is what we get paid for. The ones who would take all the anonymous glory in this secret mission would be the NRO enforcer, the FBI team and the Navy Intelligence people behind the scenes, of course. But the shadow-warriors from the Quadrille were never there....

Fullerton's men took too loading the firing tubes with 533-millimeter Mark 48 torpedoes before Jack took control of the firing mechanism embedded in his electronic wonder board, and, with every man aboard strategically placed in the cockpit, the application sailed the slick steel leviathan out of the grotto and into the river depths, beginning navigation through the Magdalena waters as we slowly left the well behind, always heading northeast. This was my first time sailing on board such a complicated craft, and, while our journey lasted, I couldn't stop feeling like professor Annorax of the Paris Museum, the famous character of Jules Verne's classic: *20,000 Leagues under the Sea*. With Jack Bull in the role of Captain Nemo, of course, and the golden albino, Norwood, as his most trusted assistant.

Once we left Colombian territory behind, we sailed slowly for hours, going from one side to another, but maintaining a general course that brought us closer and closer to the area marked as the Bermuda Triangle. It was in those waters that we finally came across the Russian Akula, waiting for us in the depths of the Caribbean Sea. The tech-spies at our naval base in Guantanamo were the first to pinpoint it. They immediately transmitted the encrypted information to the Admiralty big shots gathered at Annapolis, and from there a very special task force appointed by Admiral Seltzer forwarded the location of the Akula in direct encryption to Jack's magical board to automatically readjust its course and thus we learned exactly where the enemy was waiting for us.

Without suspecting what was coming, the waiting Russian sub commander allowed the Ohio-class to approach his vessel. When he finally realized that the American boat would not allow itself to be hooked and towed gently to the Barents Sea as previously planned, he reacted by starting defensive maneuvers that were of no use.

That's how the second Russian submarine sank and vanished.

*Refer to the fourth volume in the series, entitled *The Caribbean Sedition* (*Author's Note*).

Days later, after the operation was successfully completed — happily for us, that is — and having returned home aboard the Ohio-class submarine with its twenty-four ICBMs still intact and in perfect operational condition, I met with Col. Berkowitz, who, accompanied by Jessica, flew to the Jacksonville Naval Air Station in Florida, the largest and most important of all the naval bases located on the southeastern coast of the nation and the third most important installation in the entire country.

In a meeting that I held with him behind closed doors, he made me tell him — three bloody times, for God's sake! — *everything* that had happened since Karina and I left El Rodadero, until the moment when the Ohio-class submarine neutralized the Akula and we left it abandoned at the bottom of the ocean, like a broken toy. He recorded everything to be transferred, analyzed and filed by Jessica and said goodbye to me saying that General Cedeño and his assistant César had called to complain to him about me. When I asked him why, he replied that they were upset because I never used the satellite phone to contact them and brief them on what was taking place. This happened when he gave them the go-ahead to storm the shipyard, once Agent Norwood had informed him that I was with them on board Fullerton's vessel on the way to meet the Russian Akula. In his opinion, he added ipso facto, I had done the right thing. So, I deduced then that the matter would have no disciplinary repercussions for me.

On the other hand, Admiral Fullerton and his crew's execution, without the right to trial, before the mission was closed was well-received. And he only regretted that both Commander Ahmed and Andrei Kodina had not showed up to get their share.

"Well, it's not always possible to win them all, you know," he added in a reluctant conformist tone, "we'll deal with them another time."

The Colonel was about to leave, when suddenly he seemed to remember something and stopped.

"Tell me, Pat, what are your plans for now?" His question took me by surprise, and I did not like the fact that he had asked it in a way too intimate for my liking. Using my real name, that is, not my code name.

"As always, Colonel," I told him in the firmest tone I could manage, "I'm going to take advantage of my month's leave and go away on vacation, of course."

He pressed his lips and nodded, as if to say *I was afraid you would say so*. "Sounds good to me... Have you thought about traveling somewhere specific?"

I was tempted to answer with a *sure, where you can't fuck up my life*, but we already know that was wishful thinking.

"Probably to Puerto Vallarta, or some other nice place in Mexico," I answered.

He raised his head suddenly, as if he were a hunting dog when it sniffs a hare out in the distance and looked me in the eye. "Mexico? Why Mexico?"

"Why not Mexico? I've been wanting to go on a trip to one of its port areas to dive and fish, where they have exotic islands with beautiful beaches and big luxurious hotels with a tropical atmosphere at hand. I plan to copulate with all the gorgeous native girls I find available and drown myself in beer. Mexican beer, sir.

Nobody brews it better south of the border... Besides, to be honest, Colonel, I'm fed up with Colombia... I don't want to know anything more about General Cedeño and his well-articulated mastiff, César, and even less about Nina and Yuri. Forgive my frankness, Colonel, sir, the truth." I let a few seconds pass before deliberately adding. "But if you need me for any rising emergency...." and I left it at that, but my meaning was quite clear.

"I know, I know, don't worry. I won't be needing you soon — let's hope. You've earned your leave, soldier... I'm not going to be the one who forces you to change your plans... I'm thankful for your service. Take your leave, of course, and spend it wherever you like. But if you are determined on going to Mexico" he said that; I never mentioned the word *determined*, "talk to Mrs. Aledo as soon as you get back to headquarters. I heard she has put together an excellent vacation package for those employees who wish to travel outside the country with all kinds of discounts and benefits. It's one of the bonuses that this new Free Trade Agreement we signed with Mexico and Canada."

After this my boss left and I prayed to God, with all my heart, that I would not have to see him, or hear from him, again for the entire bloody month I had coming. Naturally, that would not be the case.

But that's another story.

THE END

ABOUT THE AUTHOR

OSCAR ORTIZ was born in 1959 (Matanzas, Cuba), but he was raised in the United States. From an early age he showed his vocation for Art and Literature and (to the same extent) his dislike for collective sports, business, science, and math. He spent his youth studying Commercial Art & Advertising. Ortiz is the winner of the "Sole Second Prize" in the **2006 ENRIQUE LABRADOR RUIZ INTERNATIONAL STORYWRITERS AWARD** with his crime story *La culpa fue de Hammett* (Blame it on Hammett) and selected "Finalist" in the **2006 TELEMUNDO WRITERS WORKSHOP** contest. He has worked as a freelance screenwriter for Telemundo Puerto Rico and Cubana de Televisión Studios in Miami. He currently resides with his wife in South Florida.